STICKY FINGERS

VOLUME 5

JT LAWRENCE

FIRE FINCH

ALSO BY JT LAWRENCE

FICTION

FUTURISTIC KIDNAPPING THRILLER

WHEN TOMORROW CALLS

• SERIES •

The Stepford Florist: A Novelette

The Sigma Surrogate

1. Why You Were Taken
2. How We Found You
3. What Have We Done

When Tomorrow Calls Box Set: Books 1 - 3

URBAN FANTASY

BLOOD MAGIC SERIES

1. The HighFire Crown
2. The Dream Drinker

3. The Witch Hunter

4. The Ember Isles

5. The Chaos Jar

6. The New Dawn Throne

STANDALONE NOVELS

The Memory of Water

Grey Magic

SHORT STORY COLLECTIONS

Sticky Fingers

Sticky Fingers 2

Sticky Fingers 3

Sticky Fingers 4

Sticky Fingers 5

Sticky Fingers 6

Sticky Fingers: 36 Deliciously Twisted Short Stories: The Complete
Box Set Collection (Books 1 - 3)

NON-FICTION

The Underachieving Ovary

ABOUT THE AUTHOR

JT Lawrence is a USA Today bestselling author and playwright. She lives in Parkview, Johannesburg, in a house with a red front door.

www.jt-lawrence.com
janita@pulpbooks.co.za

facebook.com/JanitaTLawrence

twitter.com/pulpbooks

amazon.com/author/jtlawrence

bookbub.com/profile/jt-lawrence

DEDICATION

This book is dedicated, with love and thanks,

to my Patreon supporters:

∾

Joni Mielke

Elize van Heerden

Nigel Perels

Claire Wickham

Wendy Durison

Sian Kitsune Steen

Megan Guzman

∾

Thank you also to my dedicated proofreaders,

Keith & Gill Thiele, and to all my loyal readers.

I wouldn't be able to do this without you!

STICKY FINGERS

VOLUME 5

CONTENTS

STICKY FINGERS

1

GOOD RIDDANCE

Shengdu-occupied Akeratu, 2054

Frankie cycled leisurely along the path through the midnight meadow. The air was cool on her face, and the moonlight was milky through the eternal smog that squatted over Silok, in western Akeratu. Soon the field of grey flowers was behind her, and she saw the outskirts of town. Stuttering silhouettes of the glass recycling factory, the Dairytech shop, the burned carcass of the old prison, its black ribs reaching for the sky. Before she approached the flickering streetlights, she saw Erica and slowed down. You'd be forgiven for thinking they were twins; two young girls wearing heavy coats, and breathing masks over their red lipstick, riding bikes with baskets. They squeezed their brakes and stopped beside one another, cheeks aflame against the chill of the night swirl. Erica steadied her bicycle, putting her boots on the ground, then reached into her pocket. She gave Frankie a cigarette, which the girl tucked behind her ear. With a last backwards glance, Erica placed her feet back on the pedals, and they both continued on their separate ways.

Frankie wheeled slowly into town; she was in no hurry. The Six Seasons restaurant stayed open well past dinner time. She found herself humming the resistance song—which she did when she was afraid—and immediately scolded herself and stopped.

Golden light and drunken laughter spilled out of the cracks in the double-glazed windows of the restaurant. The warm hub was incongruent against the backdrop of destruction. How do people keep living in a place like this? Working, eating, sleeping; wearing the masks that stop the acid from eating your lungs. When things before had begun to look so promising, who would have thought this would be the future? Of course, it's not like this everywhere. Across the Fiume River, the trees are still alive, and the sky is blue. The water is sweet. That's what they say, anyway; that's the whisper on the breeze. Frankie leaned her bike up against the side of the restaurant that smelled of soldiers' piss. It was darker there, and less likely to be stolen.

Frankie took off her mask and drew the cigarette from behind her ear. She read the name, written in pen, on the cigarette paper—*Bergdorf*—then struck a match and ignited the end, enjoying the quiet crackling sound it made as she dragged the fragrant smoke into her lungs. As Frankie exhaled, she thought about her mother, and her neighbour, whose bravery never failed to strengthen her resolve. Once the cigarette began to burn the tips of her fingers, she dropped it and ground it into the concrete paver under her boot. Frankie checked her lipstick in the small mirror she kept in her pocket. It had been a gift—a silver clamshell of foundation powder. It had run out long ago, but the mirror still came in handy.

The young woman pushed open the solid door of the Six Seasons, reminding herself to smile and look approachable, despite her cottonwool mouth. The warm air that rushed at her was scented with sweat and cheap alcohol: stale, but welcoming. A few of the soldiers looked up at her—those not too drunk to notice—and some continued to stare as she found herself a booth and ordered a malt beer. Frankie opened the State-stamped book she had brought along, and pretended to read while she eavesdropped on the soldiers' banter. Halfway through the drink, she had established who the high-ranking official was, and when Commander Bergdorf walked past her table, she knocked the beer bottle over, and it rolled and smashed on the floor.

"Oh!" Frankie cried, jumping up. Her cheeks were flushed. "Sorry!"

The man in his highly decorated uniform looked amused. "That's what you get," he said.

"Excuse me?"

"That's what you get for having your nose buried in a book instead of keeping us company."

Frankie appeared flustered.

"I'm only kidding," Bergdorf said. "I'd also rather be reading a good book than hanging around those bastards." He tilted his head towards his men, in case Frankie didn't know which "bastards" he meant. "Can I buy you a drink?"

She hesitated.

"It doesn't have to mean anything," he said. "I'll leave you to read in peace."

7

The beleaguered bartender came round and started sweeping the broken glass away.

"You shouldn't be drinking that cheap beer, anyway," the official said. "So, it's good riddance. In fact, if you hadn't dropped it, I would have grabbed it away from you."

The commander was charming, and his eyes glittered in a violent way that made Frankie feel nervous, and excited. "Is that what you do?" she asked him. "Grab whatever you like?"

He didn't know what to make of her. Was she criticising him, or was she joking? Was it an invitation?

"May I sit down?"

Frankie shrugged. "Sure."

Commander Bergdorf ordered a bottle of champagne for them to share. "Someone as beautiful as you should be drinking something sparkling," he said. She resisted the impulse to roll her eyes. If anything was sparkling between them, it was the wall of badges and medals on his lapel. The silver Shengdu Insignia was especially bright. Some people say the Sheng Swastika badges are moulded from the molten guns of their victims; some say the teeth.

"What do you say?" he asked, as if he had been listening to her thoughts.

"About what?"

"About this place. About life."

Frankie nudged her book aside. "There are a lot of silly stories around," Frankie said. "That's what people do when they're scared. They tell stories."

"What stories do you tell?" he asked.

"Wouldn't you like to know?" she said, a smile playing on her lips.

How ridiculous it was to sit with this handsome man and drink imported wine when she and her family had been hungry for years.

When they came to the end of the bottle, Bergdorf was drunk enough to stroke Frankie's thigh under the table, and she was drunk enough to let him. When he got too close to her secret, she grabbed his hand to stop him. His eyes burned into hers.

Frankie pulled on her overcoat. "Do you want to get some air?" she asked.

Tipsy, they stumbled out of the restaurant. Frankie fetched her bike and wheeled it alongside them as they strolled towards the forest.

"You need to go slowly," she said. "I'm not one of those Silver City girls."

His eyes flashed under the flickering streetlights. "You're worth a hundred of those girls."

He seemed more excited, then, knowing she was a virgin, and he picked up his pace.

They reached the dark woods and disappeared into the trees. The commander started to touch her, and she let her bike fall. He kissed her hard on the lips and pushed her up against the rough trunk of the tree. He stroked her through her coat, and she groaned. His fingers traced her neck, her breasts, her stomach, and then went under her skirt.

"Wait," she said, and he drew away from her. "I've got something to show you."

Without taking her eyes off Bergdorf, she began to unbutton her coat. He watched her hungrily, one by one. Once it was open, she started opening her blouse. Cold forest air made her nipples shine through her brassiére.

"You're beautiful," he said. "I don't even know your name."

Frankie reached under her skirt while the commander watched her with lust-glazed eyes. She pulled out her small revolver, and as he saw the glint of the milky moon on its barrel, she pulled the trigger three times. The trio of bullets exploded in Bergdorf's chest, and he fell backwards, his face contorted with shock.

Whenever Frankie rehearsed these liquidations in her mind, she would be cold-hearted and courageous. She'd have a line ready, something like, "Sparkly enough for you?" or "Good riddance," and then smoke a cigarette. But when it came to the actual executions, her boldness leaked away and left her shivering. Her instinct was always to help them get up.

Frankie watched as the commander's body convulsed on the dark forest floor. She had to watch them until they were motionless. Her fingers shook as she buttoned up her clothes again, and even though she tried to swallow her horror, she turned and doubled over, vomiting up the sour champagne.

The men had already dug a hole, deeper in the woods. They'd arrive in a few minutes to undress the commander and bury him. Frankie picked up her bike and wheeled it swiftly out of the forest. When she got to the outskirts, she took her compact mirror out and flashed it in the direction of where Erica was waiting, then hopped onto her bike and started to ride home. A few minutes later, she crossed paths with Erica, and they nodded at each other. This time they didn't stop.

～

"No one will suspect a young girl like you of being a resistance fighter," Erica had said, the day she had arrived to recruit Frankie. "You'll be able to make a real difference."

Frankie's mother had reluctantly agreed.

It started with distributing pamphlets and defacing Silver State propaganda. That wasn't new to Frankie; her mother had been sheltering dissidents for years. They had always collected clothes and baked bread for the Akeratu children orphaned by the war, even if it used their last sack of rationed flour. Their neighbour, Jana—a respected journalist—had been writing against the Shengdu policies for as long as she could remember. Frankie would babysit her small children, Kitsune and Milla Mouse. Jana was like an older sister to her.

After a successful mission one day—slipping past Shengdu soldiers unnoticed to deliver some explosives—Erica asked her if she wanted to save children.

"Of course," said Frankie. She loved Kitsune and Mouse as if they were her siblings. Her breath caught when she thought of them starving in a concentration camp. "Of course I want to save them."

"What is required of you won't be easy," warned Erica. "You'll hate yourself if you do it."

They took her to an underground potato shed and taught her how to shoot. She had a natural talent for it, and Erica was pleased. She gave her the powder compact and a tube of red lipstick. When she tried to give the revolver back, Erica told her to keep it.

Frankie had been confused. "How will this help save the children?"

The idea of the children in the camps haunted her. There were no photographs—of course there weren't—and no official documentation. But Jana had contacts all over Akeratu, and she told Frankie about the atrocities taking place all over the province. *Children in silver cages,* she said. *Barcodes tattooed on their necks. Gas chambers that look like showers.*

Frankie lay awake for nights on end, stomach growling from hunger, brain buzzing with the idea of the toddlers in camps. The soldiers would bang their rifle butts on the doors of adjacent houses, and the terrible sound would travel through the whole neighbourhood. First, they took disabled people—even a limp could be enough to make you disappear overnight—then homeless people, then orphans. They said they were taking them over the Fiume River, where life was more comfortable. Then when the meat rations ran out, they began shooting the cats and dogs.

"Can't they take the animals across the Fiume, too?" Frankie had asked her mother. She couldn't answer her daughter; she didn't know how.

Then Frankie understood that one day the soldiers would come for Jana's family, for Erica, for her mother, and for her. They'd bash their rifles on the door and then it would be over.

"Not without a fight," Erica said, and smiled.

Frankie smiled back and clipped her loaded revolver into the leather holster strapped to her thigh.

"We'll fight the evil our own way," Erica said, checking her lipstick in the mirror. "We'll stop the generals and the captains. We'll stop the commanders of the silver cage concentration camps. We'll fight them one liquidation at a time."

What had Bergdorf said that night when Frankie had knocked her cheap beer onto the floor? She remembered how his Sheng Swastika badge had sparkled on his lapel.

Good riddance, the commander had said. And his eyes had glittered with violence.

2

THE GENERATION OF LOST GIRLS

"What does your wife think of you paying for another woman's hotel room?"

Robin Susman knows that Captain De Villiers uses his own money to bankroll her visits to Johannesburg. The station's budget would never stretch this far.

"She doesn't mind," he lies.

In other words, she doesn't know, thinks Susman. "You'd better come in."

She steps aside, and De Villiers walks into the sparsely furnished room. There's only one chair, so he decides to stand.

"I assume the case is complicated," says Susman. "Or high profile."

He had refused to tell her what it was over the phone, which he'd never done before. Usually, she would stay well away, but they'd had a good run of luck solving the last few problem cases, and she could do with a victory in her life.

The captain hesitates.

"Spit it out, Devil," she says. "I know it's a case I wouldn't have agreed to, or you would've told me what it was on the phone."

"I know you'll get angry, but bear with me," says De Villiers. His discomfort is evident: he has new sweat-stains under his arms, and he keeps flicking the inside of his wedding ring with his thumb.

Robin purses her lips. Maybe this would be the case to ruin their run of recent successes. Still, it had come at a good time. The sheep were freshly sheared, and it would be a quiet week on the farm.

"A girl is missing," he says slowly, cautiously, as if waiting for Susman to explode.

Her expression of mild amusement melts off her face. "A girl? Do you mean a child?"

Devil rubs his stubble. "Fifteen years old."

Anger rises and flares on Susman's cheeks. "Damn you, De Villiers."

"I know," he says. "I know. It was a huge risk asking you to come out."

"Damn you," she says again, this time through gritted teeth. "I trusted you." She feels like tearing up the room, breaking something, punching De Villiers in his worry-crumpled face.

"There's something else," he says.

Susman stands there, in the middle of the hotel room, seething. "No," she says. "No. I'm going home."

"She's fifteen years old, Susman. Would you have me wait for her next birthday to ask for your help?"

"Don't be ridiculous."

"I'm not the one being ridiculous," he says, and it stings as it leaves his mouth. It burns because it's not true, and it's not fair, but he'll do what it takes to keep her on the case.

"You don't understand anything." Her eyes are shining.

"Explain it to me," Devil says. "I want to make this as easy on you as possible."

Acid drips from her laugh. "You want to make it easy on me?" She fights the urge to upend the dresser, kick the coffee table, smash the small glass mirror framed in wood. She feels fury in every molecule of her body.

"I want you to tell me how it feels."

"No," says Susman.

"I want to—"

"What?" she demands, her voice stony.

"I want to share your pain," he says. "And I want you to share mine."

Was he saying what she thought he was saying? He was telling her he loved her.

She shakes her head. "We're not doing this."

De Villiers is about to say something else, then changes his mind.

"You need to understand," she says. "You need to understand that I have to protect myself."

"Of course," he says.

"Part of protecting myself is having boundaries."

"Yes."

"No missing children. No dead children. No children, full stop."

"I know," he murmurs. "I know the rules."

"And yet here I stand in a hotel room in a city I detest—"

"I can explain."

"Do you want me?" she asks, and Devil breaks eye contact. "Do you want me around, to work cases when you need me? Then I need to be able to function, Devil. I need to be able to think clearly. Working with children unravels me, you know that. You know me."

De Villiers rubs his face again. "It's my niece."

Susman blinks at him uncomprehendingly, as if he'd just spoken in a foreign language.

"The missing girl," Devil says. "It's my niece."

"You don't have a niece," says Susman. "You're an only child."

"That's what I tell people."

"Now she's a child and a relative. That's *two* reasons to stay away from this case."

"That's the difference between you and me," says De Villiers. "I think that's two reasons to work harder than ever."

Susman snatches her handbag. On their way out, she slams the hotel door.

Susman refuses to go into the station, so they head to a coffee shop. She doesn't feel like seeing the friendly faces there, doesn't feel like returning empty smiles—and she hasn't yet decided if she's working the case or not.

"So," says Robin as she stirs her flat white. "Let me guess. You have an evil twin."

De Villiers laughs, and it diffuses some of the tension between them. "Not quite," he says. "Of the two of us, I'm the evil one. And we're not twins, just brothers."

"*You're* the evil one?" she muses. The man didn't have a wicked bone in his body, which is probably why his nickname had stuck like glue. She hadn't known him in his pre-Devil days.

"He's ... conservative. Religious. Strict with the kids."

"Too strict?" asks Robin.

"Maybe."

"You think she ran away?"

"I don't know," he says, tipping the last of his coffee into his mouth. "All I can tell you is that if I were her, I wouldn't have waited this long."

Robin fidgets with the salt grinder. "What do we know so far?"

"Dieter—that's my brother—and Magriet say she was supposed to be sleeping at a friend's house. They trusted the girl's family. They belong to the same church. They only realised Marijke was gone when they arrived to collect her and she wasn't there.

Hadn't been there at all. The family said Marijke hadn't been feeling well after school and called off the sleepover. They assumed her parents knew."

"So she's been missing since Friday afternoon?" Her mouth goes dry. It was a long time to be missing, and every hour they wasted cooled the trail.

"It's been almost 36 hours," says De Villiers, scrubbing his scalp with his knuckles. His anxiety creases his brow. "She could be on the other side of the world by now."

If Marijke was in another country, they had close to no hope of finding her.

"Blom is checking flights, passenger lists, airport footage, border control. He's also got a team kicking down doors in the city—premises of previous offenders."

Robin's stomach clenches. She bats away the picture of a fifteen-year-old girl being restrained in a dirty flat somewhere in downtown Johannesburg.

"And a search?" Susman asks.

"Khaya's taking care of that."

"A dry search?"

"For now," says Devil, and his face darkens. "Then we'll get the divers in. Why?"

Susman puts down the salt and looks the captain in the eyes.

"Please," he says to her as if she is the one who gets to decide who lives and who dies. "Please."

What could she say? She was just a damaged woman with a dry mouth.

"Robin," De Villiers says, not breaking eye contact. "Is she alive?"

At that moment, it feels like the people around them are frozen in time, and only the two of them exist.

"You can't ask me that."

"I am asking you."

"I don't know if she's alive," says Robin.

"If you had to say."

Susman looks at the captain, not blinking.

"Don't get your hopes up."

De Villiers closes his eyes and hunches over in relief. "Thank god."

"I don't know," she says. "It's probably nothing."

"Believe me," he reaches for his wallet. "It's something."

On the way out, Khaya calls and Devil puts him on speakerphone. "More girls are missing," the sergeant says. "Two more girls."

De Villiers' mouth pulls down at the corners. "What do they have in common?"

"We don't know yet," says Khaya. Working on it.

"Work harder," says De Villiers.

"Yes, Captain."

"Extend the search, and get the divers in. Rivers and lakes," he says.

"Is alive always better than dead?" Susman asks as they speed on the highway, on their way to Marijke's parents' house. She says it out loud, but really, she's talking to herself. She can't help picturing a terrified teen somewhere far from home.

"What the hell is that supposed to mean?" asks De Villiers.

It depends where she is; what's happening to her.

They drive to Devil's brother's home in the east of Johannesburg. In the suburb they visit, the front walls are low or nonexistent, not like Jozi where the homes are barricaded by brick walls and barbed wire. The houses in the quiet neighbourhood are run down, and cars and playsets rust, sinking into brown gardens. Dieter's home is neat, though. The garden is well maintained, and the house has been recently painted.

"I often ask myself why I fought so hard to survive," says Robin, as she looks out of the window. De Villiers keeps quiet as he turns off the ignition, eyes trained on the narrow tarred road.

"I would have chosen death over the attack," she says. "Why did I fight so hard?"

It's not a question either of them can answer today, not with three girls missing.

Magriet De Villiers—Marijke's mother—greets them at the door wearing a well-worn apron over an old-fashioned floral dress that reaches her ankles. The house is scented by the banana bread baking in the oven, which she serves to them, powdered with icing sugar, like a light dusting of snow.

"Thank you," Magriet says. "Thank you so much for everything you are doing to find her."

"Of course," says De Villiers.

"Your husband isn't here?" asks Robin.

"He's at church," says Magriet, wringing the tea towel in her lap. "Praying for Marijke's safe return."

"Have you remembered anything else?" asks Devil.

"I told you everything I know," she says.

De Villiers keeps quiet, letting her words linger until the woman shifts uncomfortably in her chair. She hasn't touched her plate.

Susman stands up and excuses herself, asking if she can use the bathroom. Instead, she finds Marijke's bedroom; it's as pretty as a chocolate box. Teddy bears, flowers, pink in every possible shade. The innocence—or the illusion of innocence—is almost stifling. Susman opens the dresser drawer, the closet door, looks under the mattress. Then she lies flat on the beige carpet, clicks on her penlight and searches underneath the bed. There's nothing there. But lying on the floor, she's at the perfect angle to catch a glimpse of something flashing silver from beneath the dresser. She crawls over and cranes her neck to see what's there. A razor blade is taped to the chipboard. She doesn't touch it. Taped next to it is an artful black and white photograph of a woman with protruding ribs and hipbones.

She darts into the guest bathroom and flushes the toilet, washes her hands. When she looks up, De Villiers is there.

"We've got to go," he says. "Another girl is gone."

23

. . .

Devil is pale and silent on the way back to the city.

"You're angry," says Susman. "I would be, too."

He jabs the button of the car radio to turn it on, then immediately turns it off again.

He grinds his teeth. "If it were my daughter—"

"Yes," says Robin. "You wouldn't be hiding in a church."

His knuckle-bones shine through his skin as he clutches the steering wheel.

She clears her throat. "I found a razor blade in Marijke's room."

"I was wondering what was taking you so long." He stops at a red light and swears in Afrikaans. "A razor? Why? Suicide?"

"My guess is she was self-harming. Cutting herself."

"She's not like that," says Devil.

"Like what?"

"She's a good girl."

"Good girls hurt themselves, too."

Devil's phone rings. The ringtone is classical music—Baroque? —and Susman eyes him, then answers. It's Khaya. Usually, he's cheerful, and she's never known him not to be happy she's on a case, but his voice is heavy with dread.

"Another girl?" asks Susman.

"Another girl," says the sergeant. "Also, they found something at Zoo Lake."

24

Susman puts her hand to her stomach, which suddenly aches. "Zoo Lake," she says to De Villiers. He grimaces and turns the car around.

The clouds are pink by the time they reach the lake. There is police tape cordoning off the area, and the sight of it snapping in the breeze gives Susman goosebumps. *Five girls,* she thinks. *Five girls gone.*

They approach the officer managing the scene, thinking the worst, and are relieved to learn that it's a phone that's been found, not a body—a clue, instead of a corpse. Susman glances up at the darkening sky, muttering a prayer to a god in whom she no longer believes.

"Fits the description of Marijke's phone," says the officer. "We're sending it to Betty now."

Zinzi Mbete was their go-to tech genius. She wasn't always easy to find, but if anyone could recover the data on a drowned phone, she could.

"You're sure there's no body?" asks De Villiers.

"*Yebo,*" says the officer. He also looks relieved. Maybe he has a daughter at home.

In the distance, a homeless man sits under a tree, watching them. Robin strolls up to him. He stinks of body odour and sweet wine; matches and cigarettes.

"Hi," she says. "You been here all day? Yesterday?"

He won't look at her. De Villiers approaches and hands him fifty rand, with which he seems unimpressed. Robin pulls out her wallet and peels off another hundred. He stuffs it into his jacket

25

pocket.

"This better be worth it," she tells the man. "Or I'm taking that back."

Finally, he looks up at her, his eyes stained by too much booze and living on the streets.

"There was a girl," he says, and they both stop breathing. "I thought it was a boy. Black pants, black hood. But when I called her, I saw her face."

"Why did you call her?"

"She threw her phone in the lake. I told her she should have given it to me. I need a phone. Then she ran away."

"Who was with her?" asks Susman.

"A man. I didn't see his face. He was in a car."

"Which way did they go?" asks Devil.

"Up there," says the man, gesturing up the road running up the slope, towards the main road.

De Villiers takes his phone out and scrolls through some photos. He shows the man the picture of Marijke.

"That's her."

"You're certain?" asks Robin. Witnesses are notoriously unreliable. The lake is at least thirty feet away from the tree, and this alcoholic looks half-blind.

The man nods. "It was her. I know people."

Back at the deserted station, De Villiers switches the flickering lights on and pins the pictures of the five girls to the wall, over a roughly sketched map of greater Johannesburg. According to Blom, there was no evidence they had been taken out of the country.

"So they're being held here, in someone's house, or basement."

The word "basement" made her skin crawl.

They stare at the wall. The girls were all around the same age, but that's where the similarity ended. There was no common skin colour or hairstyle. They went to different schools, belonged to various clubs, and had no hobbies in common. The phones of the other four girls had not yet been found.

"There has to be a connection," says Susman.

"It could be random," says Devil, but you can see by the look on his face that he doesn't buy it.

"Kidnapping five random girls over forty-eight hours?" says Susman. "Not likely. Not unless he had help."

De Villiers shrugs. "Maybe he had help."

At 2 AM, Devil's mobile chirruped with an email alert. Zinzi Mbete had sent him everything she had found on Marijke's phone. He opened up his laptop, and together they combed through the data which she had retrieved. There were over a thousand photos of friends, flowers, and pets.

"*Yussis,* young people take a lot of photos," mumbles De Villiers, then rubs his dry eyes and sighs as if he has the weight of the world on his shoulders.

The text messages, emails and Facebook account had all been

deleted or lost to water damage, but the names and details of the apps were recovered. SnapChat, Twitter, Instagram, Waifer.

"What's Waifer?" says Susman, and De Villiers shrugs. The icon is a pink bathroom scale. They access the application via Chrome on the laptop and log in with Marijke's details. Her dashboard loads and they see her username —CandySkull—and numbers.

Previous weight: 38kg /

Current weight: 32kg /

Goal weight: 24kg /

Ultimate Goal weight: 21kg /

On the board to the right of the numbers are pictures of skeletal looking women. Jutting collarbones and xylophone ribs.

"What the hell is this?"

"Thinspo," says Susman. "It looks like a pro-Ana app."

De Villiers' face is blank.

"It's an app that brings anorexics together. They can share numbers and tips." She clicks through to the support forum. Names like "HungryHippo" and "CalCounter" come up. CandySkull—Marijke—doesn't comment much.

Robin looks away from the screen and up at the wall with the five girls' faces pinned to it.

"They do have something in common," says Robin. "Look how thin they all are."

"The witness said Marijke looked like a boy."

Susman clicks the "groups" icon, where private chats are possible. There is only one group chat there, with seven members.

CandySkull. Coffeeandhipbones. AllCutUp. Thinskin. Slow-Suicide. Anacoach. Bonesies.

They have playful icons and lines beneath them:

Count My Ribs.

In Recovery.

The Generation of Lost Girls.

Nothing tastes as good as skinny feels.

Her pulse picks up. "This is it," she says. "This is what they have in common."

Robin's eyes track up to the pictures of the girls again. She clicks to read the chat, but the thread has been deleted.

Devil grabs his phone. "I'll get a court order."

"It's almost 4 AM," says Robin. "The judge is going to hate you."

"It won't be the first time," he says.

Susman picks up her phone, too, and dials the number she sees on the screen. It takes fifteen minutes and plenty of threats to get through to someone who can help her at Waifer.

"We don't give out that kind of information," says the American.

"One of the reasons our app is so popular is that you don't need an account to join. We don't ask for any personal details."

"But if I were to give you the usernames," says Robin, "you'll be able to tell me where they're based."

"Technically, yes, we could. But it's against our policy. We respect the privacy of every member."

If Susman could slap the man, she would. She pictured him sitting on a brightly coloured beanbag somewhere in Silicon Valley, brand new Nike Cortados on his feet, popping Adderall and slurping a large iced coffee.

"It's against your policy," says Susman, anger vibrating through her.

"Yes, ma'am," he says. "Sorry, I can't help."

She looks over at De Villiers, who is still speaking to the sleepy judge; he doesn't seem to be having much luck. She knows the link is tenuous. Her jaw begins to ache. She spits venom into the phone.

"Listen here, you bleeding-edge startup tech-wizard asshole. There are five young girls missing. They were all members of a private group on your stupid bloody app. If it weren't for your software, they'd probably all be home, safely tucked up in their beds."

"Er—"

"We're in the process of obtaining a court order. Let me tell you, when I get it, and these girls are safe, I'm going to go after you. I'm going to go after you with everything I've got. I'll find everything you're hiding. I'll strip you and your tech bare and lay your bastard bones out to dry."

De Villiers gives her a nervous look.

"And then I'm going to go to the press with this story and tell them how you wouldn't help the authorities with the investigation, and how you and your company prey on vulnerable young girls and exploit their disease for profit. And god help me if anything happens to these girls, I'll—"

"Okay," the American says. "Okay. Do you need their addresses? That's it? These seven people?"

Robin hadn't finished her tirade; she's caught mid-rebuke.

"Okay," he says. "I'll get Geoff to send them through to you now."

"Thank you," she says, then, as an afterthought: "Tell Geoff to hurry up."

De Villiers is looking at her.

Her phone pings with the data.

"Cancel that request for a court order," says Devil. "Make it a search warrant for the following addresses."

They triangulate the software developer's information with the homes of the missing girls. Five match up.

"Who are the other two?" asks Devil. Anacoach and Thinskin.

"I'm guessing 'Anacoach' is the ringleader," says Susman. "She seems the most assertive on the forum. Girls go to her for advice. I wouldn't be surprised if she organised some kind of meet-up."

"It's a flat in Rosebank," says De Villiers. "No basement."

They're both quiet for a moment.

"She could have drugged them," says Susman.

They both think *She could have killed them,* but don't say it out loud.

"Do you want to call your brother?"

"No," he shakes his head. "I don't want to get their hopes up."

They jump into the captain's old car and hurtle through the darkness. Robin's heart and lungs are rushing; she can hear her anxiety thudding in her ears. They park illegally in a one-way street and climb out onto the silent sidewalk, looking up at the apartment block with generous balconies.

"Go time," he whispers.

Robin can feel how pale she is. Her fingers tingle.

Devil looks at her. "You okay? You want to stay in the car?"

"No," she says, swallowing hard. "No way."

They ride the elevator to the seventh floor. The light inside number 78 is on. De Villiers wants to take them by surprise, so he grabs the fire extinguisher hanging in the stairwell and bashes down the door. They run in, guns in hand, shouting to get down. They expect to find the girls, drugged or bound or both, but the flat is empty. There's a sound from the balcony.

De Villiers and Susman move quickly and quietly to the large glass sliding door. The sun is just starting to rise, and the early morning breeze blows the thin curtain that separates them from the figure standing outside on the high terrace. Devil slips through the gap in the billowing voile and points his gun at the silhouette.

"Freeze," he says.

Robin is right behind him. The silhouette turns out to be an unarmed woman in smart navy blue pyjamas who looks at them defiantly. Robin catches sight of the second person too late. He's pointing a Glock G40 at De Villiers. In his other arm, he clutches a silver laptop.

"Devil!" Susman shouts. When she was trained and fit, she would have given a more useful direction, like "ninety degrees" or "gun!" but her instincts aren't as sharp as they used to be. All she can manage is to shout her friend's name—one of her only dear friends—but it is too little, too late. The gunshot is so loud in the near-silent night that it shocks her whole body, and it feels she has mercury running in her veins, her heart pumping hot and cold at the same time.

In slow motion, she turns to look at De Villiers. She expects to see him clutch his chest and fall, but instead, the woman's head comes apart and red mist sprays on the wall behind her. The man hadn't been aiming at Devil; he'd had his gun trained on the woman all along. By the time Susman has dragged her eyes back to face the smoking barrel in the dawn light, the man had leapt to his death, smashing into the concrete down below, just a couple of hundred feet from Devil's car.

Susman and De Villiers are both trembling when they get back to the vehicle. Backup and forensics are on the way. At first, they lean against the side, gathering their thoughts. It's difficult to think straight when your body is in the biochemical aftermath of shock. Susman feels numb and alert at the same time, and she can't stop moving. The morning light paints the skyscrapers silver.

"Suicide pact?"

"Looks like it," says De Villiers. He has some barely dry blood spray on his neck and shirt, but Susman doesn't comment on it. For a gut-wrenching moment, she had thought she had lost him.

The rest of the apartment had been eerily empty, with no sign of the girls. Khaya delivered the shattered laptop to Betty, but there wasn't much hope of getting anything off it except blood and metallic dust. Every hour the girls were missing meant less hope of them being found alive. After hauling the carbon monoxide scented air deep into their lungs, they open the doors and get in.

"The other address," says Susman, buckling herself in. "The seventh address. Thinskin?"

They speed towards the house in Orange Grove, not knowing what they'll discover there. They find the street—a tapered road pocked with holes. Litter swirls in dust devils outside the house, which is squat and needs its roof tiles repaired. De Villiers and Susman are still riding the adrenaline wave from the gunshots when they creep onto the property and look through the windows. The rooms appear empty. Susman and Devil look at one another; he wants to bash the door down, but they don't have a warrant. Instead, he picks the lock—which is just as illegal, but leaves less evidence. He squeezes the knob and turns it so slowly you hardly hear the spring moving, and the bolt gives way. Guns drawn, they edge inside. Susman can hear her whispered breath, and her stomach is aching again. She wonders if there is a basement.

Robin Susman doesn't want to find five dead girls. She doesn't want to find five living girls, either, if they've been brutalised. As it is, she can't sleep; her midnight mind is a spool of bad memories.

On the cream carpet in the lounge, they find the bodies. Five compact frames lying beside each other, motionless, as the rising sun slices through a gap in the drawn curtains. Susman watches them—her mouth desiccated—as Devil checks the rest of the house and comes back showing empty palms. They holster their weapons, and De Villiers coughs to clear his throat.

"Girls," he says, in his gruff way. "Girls. Wake up."

One or two of them groan. Another stretches, eyes still closed. When the blonde girl catches sight of the strangers in the room, she crawls out of her sleeping bag and onto the sofa, long-limbed and painfully thin. She looks skittish; ready to run.

"Wake up!" she yells at the others, and their eyes shoot open.

"We're here to help you," says Susman.

Marijke looks at De Villiers. "*Oom?*"

The captain is not used to being called *uncle*. He looks uncomfortable and then smiles at his niece. "You're safe, now," he says.

"What do you mean?" asks one of the girls. "Who are you?"

"We're here to take you home," says Susman.

They all frown and complain.

"We don't want to go home," says Marijke. "We all chose to be here."

"You're children," says Devil. "You don't get to decide. You belong with your parents, not some bad people you met on the internet."

"I'm not going home," says the blonde girl. "No way."

"They're not bad people!" says Marijke. "They're helping us."

Susman glares at her. "How?"

"They're teaching us how to be models. They're going to take us to New York. They've already taken some girls over there, and they say it's amazing. Sally is our coach and agent. She's organising special passports for us. Clem is a photographer, and he's shooting our portfolios."

"I know this is difficult to hear, kids," says Susman, "but Sally is not a modelling agent, and Clem is not a photographer. And I'll bet those aren't their real names, either."

"They're good people," says the blonde girl.

Devil's lips are white. "He took photos of you? What kind of photos?"

Marijke's nostrils flare, and she crosses her arms. "Nothing bad, if that's what you're thinking. He's not like that. He's kind. Kinder than *Dad*."

Blom sends them a voice message. The team in Rosebank had identified the bodies as Silje and Asbjørn Berdahl, a married couple from Norway. They're wanted in South Africa and other countries for dozens of counts of sexual exploitation of minors, human trafficking, and child pornography.

"We're going to take you to the station now, and notify your parents," says Susman, picturing Marijke's pretty room with the concealed razor blade and the photograph of jutting bones under paper skin. She looks at the scars on the girl's thin arms.

The parents would want to punish their daughters for putting them through such hell, but Susman couldn't help feeling sorry for the girls. She saw the pain on their gaunt faces. Happy kids don't make themselves disappear. Happy kids don't commit slow suicide. What were they running away from?

No, they all say. *We don't want to go home.*

"Wait for Sally to come back," says Marijke. "She'll explain everything."

De Villiers takes a deep breath. "Sally's not coming back."

～

3

AN EYE FOR AN EYE

The last thing I remember is Lorin's scream as my roadster smashes into the guardrails and flips into the air. There was Lorin's terrible wail, and then being silently airborne. Then there was nothing.

Later some bright lights shone through—hospital ceilings I guess —and doctors' terse commands. I piece together the clues I overhear. The crash, the rocks, the fire. Agony like I've never experienced before burns my every organ and bone. Pipes and palpations. Needles, catheters, and a heart monitor that sounds like a ticking time bomb. More waves of searing pain, and more darkness. A doctor with blond hair comes in and peers at me. A crucifix dangles from a silver chain around her neck. She looks familiar. She injects my IV line with something, grabs the foot of my hospital bed and navigates it out of the ward. The metal rails of the bed bump the double-doors and send a lightning bolt of pain through my broken body. I thought I might be going to the operating theatre for more surgery, but she takes me in the opposite direction. We travel down in the elevator and go outside. I see a flash of crisp sky and feel the sun briefly on my face, then she pushes the gurney into the back of an ambulance and slams the doors shut. More bumping, more agony. I try to concentrate. I want to ask where we're going, but the tranquilliser kicks in and my pain fades, along with my vision.

When I wake up, I'm in a new room. It looks like a hospital room, white and grey and clean. It has the same hospital equipment, including the ticking of the bomb. The pain is perennial. My focus fades in and out, in and out, and days pass like seconds and like centuries. The woman I thought was a doctor appears to be a nurse because she bathes me and changes the plastic bladder of my catheter. I am grateful to her, but cannot say so. I wonder why my parents haven't visited me. Do they know I'm here? I hear Lorin's scream over and over again. It is the soundtrack to my suffering. I thought the worst part of it was over, but I was wrong.

I try to talk to the blond woman who checks on me every day, but my tongue is thick, and my mouth pools with sour saliva. I have forgotten how to speak. I want to thank her and ask her to call my parents. They'll be so worried about me. I want to know if Lorin is okay.

Stravetsky, I try to say. *Lorin Stravetsky.*

My pain begins to recede, and I can breathe easier. The ticking of the bomb stabilises. I wonder if I'll ever be able to walk again.

"You're going to have a little surgery," says the woman. Her eyes are cold. She's wearing mint green scrubs and a hairnet. My body starts to shiver; I can't cope with more pain. I've had enough of the invasive medical procedures, the sharp glint of scalpels in the bright, iris-shrinking light; the scent of disinfectant. The hospital room has become my prison cell, and she's the jailer and surgeon.

She smothers my mouth and nose with a hissing mask and the air that cascades into my lungs is sweet and soporific. I try to fight the heavy blanket of black smoke that rolls towards me, but it wins. In this white sanitised prison cell, the darkness always wins.

I go to sleep with those cold eyes on me, and I wake up to the same—like ice-cubes pressed to my skin. She looks so familiar. Did I know her before the accident? I wrack my brains, but it feels like my memory has degraded along with my atrophying body. I need to get out. I try to sit up, but a new pain shears through me. I lie down; my lower back is on fire. Was that where the surgery was? Spleen, perhaps, or kidneys. I hope they were able to repair what was damaged.

There is a picture on the wall. It's a young boy, smiling. I don't know who he is. My kidneys hurt. I escape, gratefully, into sleep.

"Another little operation today," says the blond jailer with the crucifix hanging from her neck. The sweet gas soon knocks me out, and the last thing I see is Lorin's pretty face. Did I love her? I wasn't sure.

I wake up in pain. I thought I'd get used to it, but it's yet a new ache in a new place, and I think I'd rather die than go through any more of this. I glance at the door, yearning to be set free, but it is, as always, locked. There is no way to escape.

There's a new picture on the wall. This time it's a middle-aged man with a well-groomed beard. Are these people I should know? Do I have amnesia? Are we re-constructing my life?

After the next cold-eyed surgery, there are five more photographs on the wall. Seven people smile down at me as I writhe and perspire until my pillow is wet beneath me. I pull up my hospital gown—inch by inch because every movement hurts —and this time I see a fresh wound run from my shaved pubic hair up to my protruding ribcage—a neat railway line of staples. Beneath the ruptured and stitched skin, my organs ache. The woman arrives with an injection and punctures my thigh. The still air is scented by antiseptic and alcohol.

"That will make you feel better," she says, and it does. The sting recedes, and I feel as if I'm floating. I'm in the roadster as it rolls and tumbles in the air. Lorin screams.

Please, no more surgeries, I want to say, but my mouth is still not working. The woman pats me and smothers me with the mask. I've lost count of the operations I've had, but the photos on the wall give me an idea.

"You've helped lots of people," says the doctor the next time she gives me a sponge bath.

Have I? I don't remember that. In fact, I've come to realise how selfish my life has been. I was just a trust fund brat, failing class, and getting ahead anyway because of my family connections. I didn't care about anyone but myself. If I had cared about Lorin, I wouldn't have taken her for a drunken spin in the roadster after that party. It was stupid and reckless. Had I loved her? I didn't know; I guess not knowing answers the question. I was too immature to really love someone. Guilt becomes a cage I can't escape from. Ten people smile down at me from the wall.

I'm desperate to escape the cell, but it's no use. Getting out of bed and crawling to the door is excruciating and pointless. It's always locked. I know, I've tried. On one escape attempt, I left the catheter bag behind. It isn't a mistake I will make again.

The next time I wake up after being under anaesthetic, my eyes won't open. My hand shoots up, towards my head, and I feel a bandage there, wrapped around my temple. Confused and disorientated, I wrench it off, and my brain buzzes. Sharp needles of pain shoot into my eyes, which are compressed with cotton pads and surgical tape. I rip that off, too, and place my fingertips on my eyelids. That's when I start screaming. I channel Lorin's terrified scream, and we yell together like wounded animals. My eyelids are still there, but my eyeballs are gone, and only newly scarred hollows remain.

WHY? I want to scream at the surgeon. *Why?!*

My eyes weren't damaged in the crash; the surgery was not a reparative one. It was nothing less than thievery; a smash and grab. They had been pecked out by the white-lab-coated vulture.

My broken body vibrates with sobs; it hurts everywhere. I no longer have the ability to make tears. Why would she do this to me? The answer slowly reveals itself. It had begun the day I thought the doctor looked familiar. I was in denial, at first, but I slowly came to understand where I knew her from, and why she had brought me here.

I hear the lock on the door being clicked open; then I feel her presence in the sterile prison cell. I can no longer see the cheerful portraits on the wall, but I'm certain there are some new faces there. I can also feel the presence of Lorin—like a sixth sense—I picture her sitting on the foot of my bed, looking at me, her long blond hair matted with her blood.

"You've done well," the doctor says, and in my imagination, it is now Lorin who is speaking to me. "You've saved twelve people so far."

I choke in surprise, and she lifts a cup of water and a straw to my lips. "Your kidney saved an eight-year-old boy. Your section of liver saved a father of three. Your corneas gave a teenager the gift of vision for the first time."

She laid her hand on my knee. "It'll be over soon. Today is your last surgery."

I knew what that meant. After today's procedure, I would be set free.

"Do you know who I am?" she asks, and I nod, blindly. She had looked familiar because I had met her once or twice when I was dating Lorin. She was Doctor Stravetsky.

Lorin's mother, I tried to say, but it came out garbled. *And, because of me, your only child is dead.*

I hear the doctor loading up the injection and switching on the gas. I begin to shiver and sweat.

"You took my heart," she says. "Now it's time for me to take yours."

~

4

DRIVE THIS WAY FOR DEATH

Written by the (fictional) MillenniarellaBot AI after being fed classic fairytales and debate papers concerning the topic of euthanasia.

(Inspired by "The Christmas on Christmas" by Keaton Patti, who fed his bot thousands of Hallmark Christmas screenplays and then instructed him to write his own.)

～

Once upon a time, in a city bathed in moonshine soup, a voracious black wolf killed a dozen people. Some of the victims' relatives were upset; the rest were relieved. The Wolf's appetite was not sated; it never is. Wolves have stomachs that can stretch for galaxies.

A young woman dressed in a robe made of red ants and ruby ribbons made her way across the hive-like urban landscape, dodging speeding cars and men wearing FongKong sunglasses.

Her red-caped mission was to save her grandmother from the deadly wolf. She carried a basket which was woven from happy childhood memories and held black-dark forever secrets. She rushed like an autumn leaf in the snapping wind, rat-running down lonely roads and skipping over skyscrapers. A policeman stopped her with his sharp silver whistle.

"What is in your basket?" the uniformed man wanted to know, more curious than cut-throat.

"Mind your own school of sharks," she replied. When the man looked for his pistol, it was gone, and so was the girl with the basket.

The girl in the red cape had gone underground where it smelt like electricity and tar and yesterday's cream cheese bagel. The lightest bits of litter fluttered around her like abandoned moths who had found their surrogate moon.

"What is in your basket?" asked the woman on the subway. She had a giant raven's head and skin as dirty as sleet.

"None of your hot ashes," said the girl in the red robe. She was gone before the raven-woman realised her knitting needles had been stolen from her navy charity-store bag.

"What is in your basket?" asked the homeless opera singer lying on the sidewalk.

"That's for me to know," said the girl, and disappeared in a puff of red smoke, taking the singing vagrant's voice with her, and leaving just one silver coin spinning in her place.

Armed and confident, the young woman knocked on her grandmother's door. The door swung open like a haunted coffin lid.

The young woman cautiously crossed the threshold, eyeing the furniture as if it would come alive and bite her. The chest of drawers looked especially hungry.

"Grandmother?"

No one answered her but her echo; the house was as empty as a ghost's dream. She strode to the bedroom and wrenched open the moth-eaten curtains, flooding the space with starlight and dust. Her grandmother's bed was stripped bare and smelled distinctly of wolf pelt; only the old rusted-coil mattress remained. *The Wolf had already taken her,* thought the red girl. *I will get her back.*

She reached into her basket and retrieved the knitting needles, with which she unspooled the curtains and the carpet and the mattress and then spun them together. With that mismatched yarn, she knitted her way to the residence of the Wolf (more like a flying path than a magic carpet).

The Wolf's home was sleek and belonged well in the Future. There were no extras there. No excess furniture or bleak equipment or wandering souls. No, the Wolf had his business of dispatching the living down to a fine art. *Caravaggio, perhaps,* thought the girl. *Or bloody Pollock.*

The premises were so convenient it was more like a well-signposted drive-thru. Drive this way for death: white walls, bleached ivory sills, cotton clinic sheets. Come one, come all, the Grim Reaper awaits. He was down on his luck, but you just made it turn the right way around. It's the euthanasia drive-thru, roll up, roll up.

She walked to the cashier's window, which smelt of coffee stains and broken ambitions.

"That'll be one thousand koins," said the robotic waitress (who was wearing a wig).

"One thousand koins?" she asked. "To be eaten by a wolf?"

The bot gave her a polite banana smile. "Nothing in life is free."

"I don't have a thousand koins," said the girl in the red hoodie. "I can give you the pair of magical knitting needles I stole from someone on the subway."

"It's not enough," said the robot.

"I can give you a cherished childhood memory," said the girl.

"Still not enough. Don't you know that death takes everything?"

The girl used the opera singer's voice to call the Wolf with a song. He arrived, prowling in his diamond charcoal coat, his apple-seed eyes alive with all the vitality he had stolen through the centuries.

Little Red Riding Hood snatched her pistol and levelled it at the grinning Wolf; a Cheshire Cat in black dog's clothing.

Even on four legs, he was bigger than her, but the girl did not falter. "I've come to rescue my grandmother."

"You are too late," he growled, his dark lips shining. His teeth were made of carved skeletons.

The girl's eyes began to leak, but she did not lower the gun. "She's dead?"

"We're all *dead*," said the Wolf. "Life is but a pretty part-time delusion."

She shot him then, shot Death six times in the chest. She kept pulling the trigger until the chamber was empty. But as you know, dear reader, you can't kill a voracious black wolf, especially if his name is Oblivion. He absorbed the hits in elegant slow motion, and the six silver bullets became part of him; strengthening him. The pickpocketed pistol cartwheeled to the floor. The girl spun away from the advancing animal and sprinted down the white corridor, flitting like that dead leaf we had seen just minutes before.

Little Red Riding Hood found her grandmother's room. "Grandmother!"

The sick woman looked up, startled. Her eyes were pearls. She was just a fog of breath and bones; blood cells limped in her defeated veins.

The girl took her grandmother's hand; it was a cage of cartilage. "I've come to save you."

"It's too late for such nonsense," said the grandmother, like she used to say when the girl was a child and begged for one more game or bedtime story to put in her basket.

"It's not too late," said the girl. "You're still alive. You can fight the Wolf."

"You don't understand," said the sick woman. "I desire Oblivion. I've had enough living. I don't want to fight."

"I will fight for you," the girl said.

"You should mind your own pile of books," said the old woman

49

with paper skin pierced with glinting silver and invisible tubes. "This story has never been about you."

The Wolf is at the door. He lopes over and jumps up onto her grandmother's hospital bed, curling up with her. She sighs and embraces him.

"I'm not ready," said the girl. "I don't want to lose you to Oblivion."

"You are not losing me, child," the woman said with her last breath. "I will always be in your basket."

5

THE LUCKY SICKNESS

N *ote from the author:*

This story is based in the 'When Tomorrow Calls' world; it's an excerpt I adapted from the book 'The Sigma Surrogate'.

Joni clutches her stomach and hurries towards the Cloisters residence. She tries to swallow the bitter-bright lava climbing up her throat, but she's not going to make it in time.

Flickers of colour perforate her desperation: grass, petals, stones. The smell of moonflowers and compost. Above her, a cloud that looks like a centaur stretches across the sky. She races past the wrought iron gazebo with its fragrant ivory blooms trailing up the sides. Her smart sneakers crunch over the fine cream gravel of the chip stone path, spraying the small pebbles behind her. No doubt the groundswoman will mutter about it later, but Joni doesn't have time to care. Her shoes register her sudden speed and poor traction and ping a warning to her earbuttons, which she ignores.

A nut-brown rabbit with shining eyes and nervous whiskers hops across her path, and Joni almost stumbles. She knows she shouldn't be running—too much chance of falling, especially given her curse of eternal clumsiness. Running is Not Allowed here. Falling is Especially Not Allowed.

An unexpected flash of pink at the bottom of a bush catches her eye, but she can't stop to look. With her eyes off the path in front of her for that split-second, she trips, and her whole body pitches forward.

No no no no. Her body reels in slow motion. Instinct forces her hands out in front of her, and her ivory dress and palms are shredded by the tiny stones as she skids forward on them, saving the rest of her body from the impact.

The sound of the sliding gravel and her shocked breathing is loud in her ears. When she comes to a stop, she stands, places her bleeding hands on her stomach, and gives in to the terrible lurch of the Lucky Sickness.

Her stomach flips and skunky saliva gushes into her mouth. It's too late. She knows by now that when the spit streams like this —a warm sour pool in her mouth—there's no point in running any further. The best thing to do is to stop and grab a paper vombag—which she has, of course, forgotten to bring. Failing that, a bucket or a bin would do. Once, even Mother Blake's favourite yellow coffee mug, the memory of which still shames her, even though she had scrubbed it clean afterwards with bleach and a silver sponge until her hands were raw. She still blushes madly when she sees Blake drink from the thing, thinks she should steal it and smash it instead of being tormented by it every day.

Ridiculous. A smile almost reaches her lips. *Haunted by a coffee mug.*

Then any thought of laughing disappears as her stomach clenches and the vomit jets out of her mouth like an oilrig's lucky day. Joni leans over the perfectly manicured privet hedge and sprays the ground with her gastric juice. Not that there's much in her stomach: water, mostly, and some ginger air wafers that Solonne, the Surrogate Matriarx, had made her eat this morning, promising the fragrant root would help with nausea. Joni didn't want to eat them, couldn't bear the thought of anything passing her lips, but no one argues with Solonne, especially not in the communal dining room when everyone is watching. Joni had stood at her table like a recalcitrant toddler, chewing the peppery crackers, while the Matriarx nodded at her to keep going. The other SurroSisters had smiled encouragingly, despite their envy of her condition.

Fortunately, the small discs dissolve quickly—even in a dry mouth—and afterwards, Joni had been granted a walk in the SurroCloister grounds. Fresh air, and gentle exercise: that was the idea, anyway. Joni vomits again, and this time the acid stings her nose, too. Doubled over, she opens her eyes: Her white gown is scratched and stained by her fall, and the grubbiness is overlaid with fresh crimson blood-handprints, like something out of a horror film. She forces her body up again and takes a deep breath. Her hands are burning as if she'd slid over hot coals.

Why had no one told her this would be so difficult?

"It will be fun, they said." Joni wipes her mouth and her nose on the back of her hand, muttering away to herself. "It'll be an adventure. You'll be saving the future! It's the most respected job in the country!"

She picks up her copper 'SS' pin that had fallen onto the emerald grass and pins it back over her heart with trembling fingers. She swallows the next heave, and this time it stays down. The worst is over, for now.

It's all kind of true, and the perks *are* awesome, but when you feel this sick for this long, well, no amount of money or respect can really make you feel human. Her body is swollen, her brain is fluff, her mouth is a devil's ashtray.

Gingerly, Joni makes her way back towards the gazebo. She can use the rainwater fountain there to flush away the bitterness and rinse her grazed skin; then she'll head to the matron for some antiseptic plasters and a scolding. The idea of the cool, clean water pushes her reluctant limbs forward. Her smart sneakers ping green: They are happy with her pace now.

We are definitely living in the future when your shoes double as your nanny.

She sees the flash of pink on the ground again, and this time, she stops to look at it.

Oh!

It looks like her fortune is finally turning. At the foot of the hedge, cushioned by a clump of sweet Mexican daisies, is a giant easter egg, most likely left over from the Spring Hunt on Sunday. Easter is always a big deal here. Not the scary Christian version, obviously, but the original Pagan *Ēastre,* celebrating new life and the rite of the northern hemisphere's spring. Even the perennially cross Mother Blake had gotten into the spirit, wearing a crown of chamomile blossoms and diving for choxo-late eggs, which had made all the sisters giggle.

The hollow candy egg is the size of an ostrich's and is made of the palest pink sugar sand, with vintage vanilla lace detail. The scent of imitation strawberry ice cream is subtle but takes her back in time to when she was a small child: a yapping black poodle, a chintz couch. Sitting on her mother's lap while she knitted blanket squares for the local orphanage. That's when orphanages still existed. Most of Joni's school friends wouldn't even know the word, now. She inhales the comforting scent deep into her lungs. Why is the sense of smell so nostalgic?

Joni holds the delicate egg in her burning, bleeding hands like a hard-won prize. A precious gift from the universe to signal that everything is going to be okay. The Lucky Sickness will pass, she'll be able to complete her job and move back home. Her life will be—relatively—normal again.

Besides, what is normal, nowadays? 2021 is the year of the blight, despite what the UN wants you to believe. Relentless drought; intractable corporate corruption; the Superbug; the Suicide Contagion. And, of course, the reason she's living in this strange gated community: a devastating infertility crisis. When her over-protective parents told her she'd be safest living here in the Cloister instead of at home, she had railed against them, accused them of abandoning her. But when she glimpses the news headlines on Mother Blake's Tile or hears the hard-whisper bedtime gossip of the other girls, she knows her parents were right to offer her to the SurroTribe as a recruit.

Even if she had an appetite, Joni decides that the Easter egg is much too pretty to eat. Inspecting its delicate icing, she notices that the egg has a seam: The top and bottom can twist open. There'll be a surprise gift inside. She's torn between seeking the water she's craving and opening the shell. Before she reaches a decision, she swivels the egg, and as it opens she sees a couple of wires attached to something that looks like a battery and some silicone clay, and then there is a loud explosion, and the hot force of it hits Joni in the chest and jaw, and knocks her flat on her back. Joni's last thought, as she lies on the grass, ears chiming, is how very young she is, how short her life has been ... and that Solonne will not be very happy. So much for luck.

Drought, crime, suicide, and an Easter egg.

Of all things to be killed by.

She watches the cloud centaur pull back his arrow, and then her vision fades to a blip.

Thi*his story was originally written as a play and optioned by the national broadcaster, the SABC.*

~

Welcome to the lesser-known country of The Kingdom of Moldavia, known for its overgrown jungles, giant pineapples, venomous bronze-fanged adders, and the finest butterfly silk in the world. It's home to tigers so ferocious and so vain that the only way to survive an attack is to dangle your pocket mirror in front of their trembling fish-gut whiskers. It's a place where fire-bugs will put on a pyrotechnic show for you and, while you are watching, the satin-smooth hands of vervet monkeys will swipe your wallet. There are mountains of silver here, and gold, and diamonds fall like rain (if you stand in the right place at the right time).

There is also blood. Old, black blood that has leaked into the soil for centuries, fertilising the land with the life it has recycled. There is thick brown blood that coats the pebbled roads, sticky enough to provide the traction needed for progress. And there is violet blood. New, gushing violet blood that is pumped by love and lust and excitement through the peoples' veins by their purple piston hearts.

I'm glad you could join us. This story—as all good stories are—is about ADVENTURE. I'll be your guide, your translator, your—

Two armed men scuffle in the castle hall. There is pushing and punching, gasping and groaning. Weapons are drawn: a scimitar and a loaded pistol.

King Zam presses the scimitar into The Baron's throat. "I've got you by the balls, now, you scoundrel!"

"Well, technically, you have me by the throat," whispers the Baron. "My balls are located in another place entirely."

"Excuse me, gentlemen," I say. "I'm not quite finished the introduction yet—"

"I am the Baron of Balaclavia! I need no introduction."

"And I am the King!"

I watch them wrestle. "Yes, yes," I say, "but the story doesn't start here! We need to go back. Sixteen years into the past."

"Sixteen years!" exclaims the Baron. "In that case, Your Royal Highness, could you do me the kindness of lowering your emerald-studded scimitar from my adam's apple?"

"It's a reasonable request. I'll do so, but only if you remove your ivory-handled pistol from my belly."

They glare at each other one last time, then lower their respective weapons.

"Shall we have a drink, while we wait?" asks King Zam. "Sixteen years is an awfully long time."

That would be smashing," says the Baron. "Much obliged."

The king claps his hands for service, and a mousy servant arrives.

"Putin! Bring us some warm brandy. The one from Xonofi. Use the snow-crystal snifters. Have you heard of it, Baron?"

Putin hurries over to the drinks trolley and begins to prepare their drinks.

"Of course," says the Baron. "It's arguably the best brandy in the world! Made from baby ruby grapes found only on the highest hills in the forests of Lanau, fermented in hundred-year-old oak barrels and seasoned with the happy tears of the vegan Veranova virgins."

King Zam looks impressed. "That's the one."

Putin hands them a glass each, and they clink snifters and wish each other excellent health and happiness.

Sixteen years prior, in an abode far less handsome than this particular castle with its alabaster turrets and snake-skin ceilings, a woman was lying with her legs open on a straw-mattress bed. She was screaming blue murder—

"You can do it, Sharoni, you can do it," said the midwife with baseball mitts for hands. "Let's have one more push. Give it all you've got."

Sharoni strained and screamed as she used all the strength in her body to push.

I daresay that you would be screaming too if you were giving birth to a baby as buxom as the Baron.

"His head is out!" shouted the midwife. "One more push, love."

The baby made his appearance and gave a lusty yell.

"It's a boy!" announced the midwife.

"He's beautiful," said Sharoni. "Isn't he beautiful? He has his father's handsome chin!"

The midwife nodded enthusiastically. "I've never seen a more beautiful baby."

That's what the midwife told every new mother—even when Mrs. Borgione up the hill gave birth to a sprog who looked more like an orang-utan than a daughter. The midwife weighed the baby and mutters to herself.

"What is it?" asked Sharoni, lifting herself onto her elbows to see.

"He's a record-breaker, by the looks of it."

"What do you mean?"

"He weighs 68 pebblestone!" She wrapped the infant in a soft muslin receiving blanket that had seen a dozen babes before him. The midwife had boiled it in sweet streamwater with dandelion flowers and let it dry in the shade. "He's a big boy, that's for sure."

"Yes. Yes, he is," Sharoni cooed as the midwife handed her baby over. "He's destined for big things."

And so The Baron was born. Of course, he wasn't always called The Baron. He named himself that after he taught himself to read using a moth-eaten encyclopaedia and some sticks of charcoal he found in the backyard. Once he knew how to read, he combed the village and devoured any book he could get his hands on, but one book, in particular, captured his imagination like a grizzly in a bear trap. Look at him now, sitting before the fire crackling in the hearth of his village home, his head buried in the well-thumbed pages.

"You're not reading that Baron book AGAIN, are you, darling?"

"I am," announced the boy. "I read it every day. I think I've read it a thousand times already and I'll read it a thousand times more."

"I don't know how you find the time! With all your golden-mongoose hunting and salt-river swimming and rescuing fallen chicks from under their tree nests."

"I'm starting archery tomorrow. Mr. Beeswax said he'd teach me."

"Well, just be careful, please."

"You always say that."

"And you'd do well to remember it."

Indeed, with his fearless spirit, The Baron often got himself into sticky situations. When he was five years old, he started a fire in the neighbour's barn. The village men rushed to put the fire out, and pulled on his sooty ears for causing a ruckus—

"I was just trying to melt some raven feathers—" he said.

"Melt some raven feathers?" exclaimed one of the villagers. "Have you gone mad?"

The owner of the barn began to take off his belt, but his company stopped him. "I almost lost four seasons of straw! In these hard times! You deserve a good whipping, boy!"

"Go easy on the lad," said the blacksmith.

"He's a mischief maker!" yelled the neighbour. "He needs sorting out!"

"He needs a father figure!"

"Someone to tan his hide, you mean?"

"A good thrashing will fix him!" shouted the neighbour, his cheeks as red as ripe nectarines. "My father would have belted me all the way to Jupiter!"

"He 'fixed' you, did he? And look how you turned out!"

The villagers laughed—a little too loudly.

"Besides," said the blacksmith. "He burnt his little paws trying to put the thing out. It's punishment enough for the poor mite."

"I thought," said the young Baron, "if I could melt some feathers together, then the thing I'd have made would be able to fly."

The men laugh again, but this time there is affection in it. One of the villagers tousled the boy's hair.

"You're a dreamer, alright. You've got little firecrackers in your brain. You'll become someone, that's for sure. He'll become someone, mark my words."

∿

A year later, the Baron traipsed into the wild jungle with nothing but his favourite book, a handkerchief filled with almond biscuits and his folding hunting knife, and didn't return for six nights. He left a note for his mother, telling her not to worry, but as all mothers know, it's impossible to do, especially if you are the mother of a 6-year-old intrepid adventurer. As all mothers know, having a child is like having your heart skipping outside your body, raw and vulnerable to the thundering elements. Sharoni slept outside the house every night he was gone and saw his face in the stars. It was the only way she could know that he was still alive and adventuring, and not inside the belly of a tiger. On the seventh day, he returned: taller; thinner; much, much dirtier; and with an animal attached to his shoulder. He ran towards Sharoni and hugged her legs. She smacked him upside the head, then hugged him harder than she had ever before.

"Ouch!" exclaimed Marcus Pointdexter, the animal on the boy's shoulder.

Sharoni held onto the boy's arms and pushed him away just enough to see the creature. "What now? Who are you, then?"

"This is Marcus Pointdexter," said the boy Baron. "He's my pet lemur."

"I prefer the term 'companion'," said the animal.

"A monkey?" asked Sharoni.

"A lemur," said the boy. "A talking lemur."

Pointdexter smiled in a Cheshire Cat way. "The best kind there is."

"You found him in the jungle?" she asked.

The Baron shook his head. "He found me."

"It was the almond biscuits that did it," said Pointdexter. "I never have been able to turn down an almond biscuit."

Sharoni lifted the boy's chin with her finger, to inspect it. "And what happened to your cheek?"

"It's nothing. It's almost healed. I used Eucalyptus leaves on it, and a tincture of saffron and sage."

"It was an unfortunate canoeing incident," said the lemur.

"The canoe cut your cheek?" she asked. "Or a rock, perhaps, in the rapids?"

"It was a wrestling match with a forty-foot crocodile with filthy yellow daggers for teeth."

Sharoni's face paled. "A crocodile?"

"Don't worry, Mama. It wasn't that big. Marcus Pointdexter is known to exaggerate."

Then, at 6, there was the infamous horse accident, when the Baron jumped on the rose-petalled back of a wild stallion to go for a ride—which went well until they galloped under a particularly low-hanging branch of a popping pepper tree that stuck the young boy in his left eye.

"I like my eye-patch," said the young Baron, snapping his book shut. "It gives me character."

"It's a wonder you can read at all, with one eye," said his mother.

"One eye is all you need! I'm off to archery practice."

"Well, take your big brother with you."

The boy looked confused. "Dash?"

"Yes, Dash. Do you have any other old brothers that I don't know about?"

"Take Dash? To play with arrows? Are you sure?"

"You know how he loves being included," said Sharoni. "How he looks up to you. It'll be good for him. It'll get his head out of the clouds."

The years passed quickly, like rocks rolling down the hilly green landscape of mossy southern Moldavia. Despite various colourful stunts and capers, the Baron's thirst for adventure was never quenched. He longed to leave his quiet village in search of a crusade.

"A crusade for what?" asked Dash. The two brothers were standing on the bank of a stream, fishing for blue-scaled lobsters and skimming pebbles.

"What do you mean?" asked the young Baron.

"You say you want to go on a crusade. What kind of crusade? For what purpose?"

"It doesn't matter!"

"What do you mean, it doesn't matter? The whole point of a crusade is to do something for a reason."

"I don't need a reason," said the Baron. "It'll be an adventure!"

"Ha."

"Ha?"

"Meaningless adventure. Where will that get you? What's the point?"

"You think too much. Adventure is the point, egg-head!"

"What about the rest?" asked Dash.

"What else is there?"

"Success," chipped in the lemur, yawning. "Money. Love."

"Hello, Marcus Pointdexter," said the Baron. "I didn't see you there."

"I was asleep. In the knapsack."

The Baron looked at his brother. "Will you look after Ma? You know, when I'm gone?"

"So you get to go off, and I'll be stuck here, in this dead-end village? What will I do? Apart from my blasted ironmonger apprenticeship? Do you know that the ironmonger has a serious case of halitosis?"

"You don't have to. You can come with us!"

"Who is 'us'?"

"Marcus Pointdexter and I, of course."

"Go on a pointless adventure with my little brother and his pet lemur?"

"I prefer the term 'companion'," said Pointdexter.

"It'll be a blast. What do you say?"

Dash threw a pebble into the stream. "I'd rather take my chances with the ironmonger."

So the Baron planned his trip, drawing a map of Moldavia on the hide of a yellow buffalo with chalkstone and the juicy wax of lipstick corn. The whole village helped, pointing out what they knew of the lay of the land from their limited journeys to collect stock and capture errant daughters.

"This part here, Dudlin, in the west," said one of the villagers. "It's much bigger than that. And there's a giant waterfall here ... that flows backwards, up the mountain. Man-eating goblins live behind the 'fall, so don't go anywhere near it."

The butcher stepped in and sketched a lake. "I'm adding in the Fuerté Lake. In the east, here. It's filled with warm, copper-coloured water."

"That sounds beautiful," said the young Baron. "I'd like to see that."

"Stay well away, lad!" warned the butcher. "It's teeming with pirañas and aqua-sequinned mermaids that will drown you if you give them a chance."

They all crossed their arms and nodded. *Aye, aye. Best to stay away.*

"You must also give a wide berth to the golden grasses of Shamrocky, here, in the centre," said the baker, jabbing the map with her flour-powdered fingers.

"Aye, those leaves are razors," agreed her husband.

"Those grasses will slice you quicker than the King's emerald-studded Scimitar."

"So," said the boy. "I should avoid the east, the west, and the centre of Moldavia."

They all nodded and agreed.

"So ... I'll go to the north, then."

"Oh, no," they clucked. "Oh, no, no, no."

"That's not a good idea," said the blacksmith.

The old neighbour piped up; his frown etched forever into his face. "Don't you know anything, boy?"

"I'm not a boy," said the young Baron. "I'm a man!"

The villagers all laughed.

"You may have a beard and a broken voice, lad," said the neighbour, "but you're not yet twelve."

"What's in the north, then, tell me?"

The villagers danced on the spot, all keen to tell him.

"The king!" said the butcher.

"King Zam," said his wife.

"The ruthless, reckless, bloodthirsty king."

"The Remorseless Ruler of the Kingdom of Moldavia."

"He's more dangerous than all the rest, combined! Him and his savage soldiers. They'll not hesitate for a moment before shooting you full of arrows. Men come out of there looking like porcupines—"

"Dead porcupines."

"Very dead porcupines. If you somehow manage to dance

around those arrows, then the army with flintlocks will be waiting for you, and after them the blunderbusses and the cannons and the boiling oil."

"His castle is clad in alabaster white enough to blind you when you approach."

"There is a thorny maze of poisonous snickerbushes all around the castle. It can take days to find your way through it. But no-one ever does, because they either starve halfway through or eat the deadly snickerberries."

"It's a bad way to die. A very bad way."

They nodded and gave each other sincere looks of understanding.

"If you get through the maze—which you never will—you'll be faced with a moat alive with the long snapping jaws of gharials."

"I can fight them!" said the boy. "... What are they?"

"Gharials are narrow-snouted crocodiles, son, the meanest kind. And the king keeps them hungry."

"He can definitely fight them," piped up Marcus Pointdexter. "He once fought off a 40-foot crocodile."

The villagers chuckled and hooted and stomped their feet in amusement. The baker was laughing so hard she crossed her legs and looked as if she needed the privy.

"I did, too!" shouted the one-eyed boy. "I did fight off that crocodile!"

"Ah, we know, son," said the blacksmith.

"Then why are you all laughing?"

"It's the talking monkey! He cracks us up every time."

On the day of his departure, the Baron shook everyone's hands while Sharoni wrung her hands and wept.

"Good luck, son," said the blacksmith.

The cantankerous neighbour's voice was gruff with emotion. "Try to stay out of trouble, now."

"Send us word every now and again, if you're able, just so that we know you're alive."

The young Baron kissed his weeping mother and hugged his sulking brother. With a happy wave from the boy and Marcus Pointdexter, they began their journey into the wild country of Moldavia.

They walked for a year, hiking over thorny mountains and wading through sharp-stoned rivers where the water ran cold and sweet. They walked till the Baron's shoes were worn through—which he had grown out of, anyway—and was glad to see them stolen by a pair of mischievous ginger squirrels on the eve of his 13th birthday. Every month at full moon, he sent a raven back to his village, with a gift for his mother: a fistful of golden pomegranate jewels; a dried fig; a rock polished smooth by the rushing rapids. A sprig of rooted lavender; a pretty flower fossil; an old kidney bean engraved with a heart. Never had such simple gifts been more happily received: each one a parcel of evidence that her son was still adventuring.

. . .

When they reached the sea on the western-most tip of the country, The Baron knew that the first leg of his journey was over. They could hear waves crashing and watched as gulls wheeled overhead.

"Look at that, Pointdexter! I've never seen the ocean before."

"Is this it, then?" asked the talking lemur. "Will we go home now?"

The Baron picked up a clamshell. "Do you want to go home?"

"No," said Marcus Pointdexter.

"Good, because I have a feeling our adventure has only just begun."

"What makes you say that?"

"There's an especially ugly man-eating beach goblin standing right behind you."

So far, The Baron had fought off a diamond-skinned python, a ten-legged albino forest spider, and a rabid raccoon that tried to kidnap Marcus Pointdexter. He had never, however, brawled with an especially ugly man-eating beach goblin.

"Now, listen here, Goblin," said the young Baron. "I know what you're thinking, and you're wrong."

The goblin looked at the boy, his mouth watering. "Ooga?"

"You're thinking how tasty we look. But we're not."

"Ooga."

"Look here," said the Baron, lifting his threadbare shirt. "There's no meat on me. See? Skin and bone, I am." He slapped his ribs to accentuate his point. Unfortunately, this had the opposite of the desired effect, and the goblin began to salivate more.

The boy lowered his shirt again. "I'd just be a waste of your dinner fire."

The beach goblin took a step forward and licked his rubbery lips.

"I'm not sure your argument is having quite the desired effect," said Marcus Pointdexter.

"Ooga!"

"He's pointing that way," said the boy. "I think he wants us to go with him."

"Of course he wants us to go with him! Much less work for him if we walk to his cave before he brains us with that club and throws us in his mussel pot."

"Come on, then." The Baron began to follow the goblin, who looked mightily pleased with himself.

"You can't be serious," said the lemur, who was being left behind on the empty beach. "You'll end up as bouillabaisse! Or worse: ceviché!"

The Baron yelled so that Pointdexter could hear him. "I want to see the waterfall that flows backwards!"

"It'll be the last thing you ever see! They'll batter you!"

"I can handle a battering," said the boy.

Marcus Pointdexter ran to catch up with the pair. "No, I mean, they'll batter you and deep fry you! They'll Surf & Turf you!"

"Well, are you coming?"

Pointdexter straightened his spine as if brushing off an undeserved insult. "Of course I am."

Soon they approached the magnificent—and deadly—Dudlin waterfall.

"Spectacular!" exclaimed the young Baron. "Look at that waterfall! It really does go backwards! I've never seen anything like it in my life!"

Marcus Pointdexter nodded. "Made all the more poignant by the fact that we're about to die."

"The majesty of it," said the boy. "The power!"

"And just behind the watery curtain: a hundred hopping hungry beach goblins who want to boil us for brunch."

The goblin who had lured them there nodded, hopped on one foot, and salivated. "Ooga!"

They followed him into the cave behind the gravity-defying waterfall.

"Holy Moldavia!" exclaimed Marcus Pointdexter. "What is that stench?"

"Old fish bones," said The Baron. "Sun-dried sharkskin leather. Rotten calamari."

"Not that. The OTHER smell."

The boy sniffed the air. "I think that's the goblins."

"But I don't see any—"

Just then, the shining, glowing, blinking eyes of a hundred slimy beach goblins came out of the shadows. "Ooga."

The Baron and the lemur took a step back and resisted their impulses to pinch their noses shut against the terrible smell. The goblin who had brought them to the cave began to address the crowd. He spoke in a rude-sounding guttural language that the boy nor his companion understood. The group, however, liked what they heard and cheered.

"Well!" said the young Baron. "This is going better than I expected."

The riot of goblins rushed straight for the Baron, and Pointdexter screamed. The goblins lifted them both into the air and began singing a cheerful-sounding song. The lemur stopped shrieking. "Wait, what?"

For a reason unbeknown to the travelling pair, the goblins were celebrating them: lifting them in the air, kissing their ankles, licking their knees, and singing them goblin pop songs.

"Do you think this is some kind of pre-slaughter ceremony?" whispered the Baron.

"Probably," said Pointdexter. "But it's fun, nonetheless."

Instead of the goblins carrying them to the fishbone fire, they hoisted the pair to a high wall deeper inside the cave, which was illuminated by scores of whale blubber candles. The goblins set them down gently, and the goblin with the club tapped it against the cave wall. There was a slight echo. "Ooga."

Another goblin holds a fiery torch up to the wall.

"He's trying to tell us something," said the boy. "Through the rock art."

"Let's see," said the lemur, trying to follow the story drawn on the wall. "This is a woodland elf, next to a tree. He has dark hair and a creepy smile. This is a very ugly monkey. And a large dragon is about to cuddle them. I think it's the goblins' rather naïve supernatural interpretation of a Shakespearean sonnet."

"That is not an elf," said The Baron. "And that dragon is not about to cuddle them. Look at his massive jaws, his dirty, dagger-y teeth. In fact ... he looks quite familiar."

Pointdexter moves to look at the painting on the left. "The dragon's here, too, in an earlier story."

The Baron joins him and squints at the illustrations. "He's ferocious here. He's just destroying everything. And look—"

"He's gobbling up the goblins!"

The goblins began hopping up and down again, chattering in excitement.

"Hundreds of them," said The Baron.

"Ooga!"

"But the elf and the monkey—"

"The dragon bit the elf's face—"

"But then the two slew the dragon!"

"And look here. Look how happy the goblins are. They're—"

The goblins cheered and danced.

"It's not a dragon at all, Pointdexter," said The Baron. "Not a woodland elf. Not an ugly monkey."

"What now?"

"It's us! It's a child and a lemur. And that's the crocodile we fought! That's my scar! We chased away their mortal enemy."

"But ... that was so long ago. So far away. How did they know?"

"Stories. Gossip. Rumours. Broken telephone. The same way we heard about them."

And with that, the chief beach goblin handed The Baron an extraordinary gift. It was a small skeleton of a fish, white and polished, and fully intact. The Baron thanked him and hung it on a leather cord around his neck. He didn't know exactly what he would need it for, but he had the feeling it would come in handy.

"Thank you, sir," the boy said, bowing down to the gabble of goblins, and they parted to allow The Baron and Marcus Pointdexter to continue on their journey.

Twelve moons later, the pair of travellers reached the centre of Moldavia. During the journey, the Baron had sent his mother 12 raven-gifts, including a round sea-sponge, a pouch of vanilla tobacco, and a red crayon made from the gum of the rare ScarletSap tree. It had been a challenging walk, but The Baron had taken time out to rest and make himself new clothes when his others fell off. His shirt was cotton, woven from the green Gossypiums that embroidered the westward paths they had taken. His pants were silk, made from a thousand cocoons he had collected from under the leaves of purple-blooded mulberries. He was especially proud of his belt, a special kind of rubbery leather, made from the pelt of a kangaroo that he had hunted with his whittled-cinnamon arrows. He had also fashioned a rainproof hooded jacket and a pair of sturdy shoes. The marsupial meat he had divided: he roasted the ribs with green wasp honey over a rosemary wood fire, and shared it with a passing shepherd who told him of unrest in the North.

"The people are planning a coup against the king!" said the travelling man. "They've grown tired of his careless and evil ways. They're starving. They're digging up frozen potatoes to eat. They're dressing their children in rags while the king flounces around in gold-trimmed velvet."

The rest of it, he cut and cured, and made into smashed-coriander biltong (the kangaroo, not his dinner guest).

The pair tried to avoid Shamrocky, the golden grasses of the interior they had been warned about, but there seemed to be no access to the West without entering the fields of razors.

"Look at how it shimmers!" exclaimed The Baron. "How the breeze makes it come alive."

"It'll cut us to ribbons!" said Marcus Pointdexter.

"Then at least we'll die in the most beautiful place in the world."

The lemur may have whimpered.

"We either brave the golden glade, or we go home."

And so the Baron lifted Marcus Pointdexter on to the top of his head, where the blades could not reach him. He wore his kangaroo skin as he waded through the sharp plants, and, after seven days, emerged with only seven hundred cuts, instead of the expected (and fatal) seven hundred thousand. He was weak, and his skin was on fire, but an unscathed Marcus Pointdexter bathed his wounds in oak sap and camomile tea, and by the next day, he was fit to walk again. The Baron harvested some of the brilliant grass, and at the full moon, he sent half the bundle with a raven to his mother. The rest, he kept in his knapsack. It was time to head to the westernmost point of Moldavia, and the warm-as-bathwater Lake Fuerté.

The Baron was fifteen years old by the time they reached Fuerté. Again his clothes had fallen off him, but this time he had not replaced them. The winds of Fuerté blew hot and carried the aroma of nutmeg reeds and healing mud, and he liked the feeling of the sun on his skin, which turned his body a beautiful burnished mahogany that would never fade for as long as he lived. He no longer needed shoes; his feet now had their own leather. When The Baron and Marcus Pointdexter saw the gentle lapping lake—the expanse of welcoming water—they forgot all mention of the pirañas and dangerous mermaids, and dove into the copper-coloured sea.

"I need to stay here where it's shallow," said the lemur. "I can't swim! And you can stop tickling me now."

"I'm not tickling you."

Marcus Pointdexter let out a shrill laugh. "I mean it, Baron! Cut it out!"

"I'm not doing anything!"

"Stop!" giggled the animal. "Stop!"

The baron lifted his hands out of the water. "Look, here are my hands. They're nowhere near you."

The lemur frowned. "But ... then ..."

Before he could finish his sentence, he was pulled sharply under the water.

"Pointdexter?" called The Baron. "Pointdexter? Stop kidding around." He couldn't help feeling scared. He took a deep breath and dove down into the water, trying to find his friend. He went under again and again, but Pointdexter was nowhere to be found. Just as the Baron was about to pass out from lack of oxygen in his desperate rescue attempt, something magical happened.

The underwater world of Lake Fuerté came alive. There was music, harps played by beautiful mermaids, and singing. They smiled at The Baron and beckoned him closer. Their long hair flowed in the gentle currents of the water.

"Baron!" said the mermaid with red hair. "We've been expecting you."

"We're so glad you're here," said the one next to her, with shimmering pale blue scales.

"Where's Pointdexter?"

The mermaids parted to show him the lemur, who was relaxing with his paws behind his head. He sighed happily. "Don't mind me."

The mermaids were feeding Pointdexter peeled sea-grapes and massaging his lemur toes.

"What is this?" asked The Baron. "Am I dead? Have I drowned?"

The mermaid with red hair laughed. "You humans are always so paranoid."

"Just relax," said the other. "You've come a long way. Sit down, let us pamper you. You deserve it."

"I was told about you," said The Baron. "That your beauty is enough to drown a man."

The redhead laughed again. "Well, that may be true."

The other one tittered. "He's not just handsome—just look at that chin!—he's charming, too!"

"I've heard that you have drowned legions of men," said The Baron. "That this river sand is made up of the crushed skeletons of generations of Moldavians."

"If you think that is true, then why are you not afraid of us?" asked the mermaid.

"How do you know that I'm not afraid?"

"Because it is the fear that drowns the men. Not us."

"Not unless we choose to, anyway," said the one feeding Pointdexter, and there is the tinkling sound of mermaid laughter, like seashells on a wind chime.

"And why do you choose not to drown me?" asked The Baron.

"You were kind to our father, who you passed a year ago, in Shamrocky. He was hungry, and you shared your meal with him."

"Besides, you're too handsome to drown," said the mermaid with the blue scales.

"Your father? The only person I met there was a travelling shepherd."

The women laughed again. "Sometimes he travels as a shepherd. Sometimes a cobbler. He finds his merman tail is not practical for long journeys on land and relies on the kindness of strangers. His job is an important one: to spread the word of the ruthless king, who eats gold while the children of Moldavia starve. You helped him do that."

"We'd like to thank you," said the mermaid massaging Pointdexter, who had all but passed out from the pleasure. "Let us take care of you."

A new mermaid, this one with blonde hair, swam up with a tray of refreshments.

"Here, have some caviar, and some sea-berry wine."

The redhead begins to rub his shoulders.

"Oh, that's good," said The Baron.

"Now, just let yourself go..."

As the Baron began to relax, a white fish darted towards him and whispered in his ear.

"Don't fall asleep!"

"What?" asked The Baron, his eyelids heavy. "Why?"

The fish dashed away again. Luckily, in a moment of clarity, the Baron understood the fish's message. If he fell asleep, his bones would join the skeleton-sand that was underneath him.

"Pointdexter!"

The lemur was practically comatose. "Uh-huh?"

"Don't fall asleep! If you fall asleep underwater, you'll never wake up."

"That's true," said the mermaid with the siren-red hair, cocking her head. "But don't take it personally—"

And the Baron didn't, because he knew that no one could deny their true nature, least of all mermaids.

When the pair of travellers had enjoyed their share of lake luxuries, and their bodies were sated and revived, they surfaced to the cornflower sky and dried off in the sun. The mermaids had been reluctant to let The Baron go, but when he insisted, they had kissed him with their briny pink lips and given him a parting gift: a tightly stitched nori leaf suit, with mermaid scales of armour.

"The other lemurs are never going to believe me when I tell them about *that*."

"It did feel like a dream. I can see how some men don't come out alive."

"The mermaids were very ... shall we say ... *persuasive*."

"But we have things to do! Places to be!"

"What? Where?"

"The North, of course! Where else? We have a kingdom to conquer."

In the time it took the intrepid adventurers to get from Fuerté to the edge of the Purple Pines—the forest bordering King Zam's castle—the Baron had sent his mother the following gifts: An adder stone; a whitewood bonsai sapling; a pouch of cumin incense; an abandoned starling's nest with a single speckled egg inside; and a hairbrush made of purple pine needles. The egg may not have made the journey intact; ravens can be mischievous like that.

They came across a glade—a clearing in the forest—where a dozen ramshackle houses stood. The Baron was about to call out his greeting when a rather large rifle appeared at his temple, and the safety catch was flicked off.

A man with a mask yelled at them. "And what have we here? An intruder! A pirate! A spy!"

The Baron remained calm. "We come in peace."

"Ha! That's exactly what a spy would say! Put your hands up, or I'll blow them off!"

"That seems a little brash," said Marcus Pointdexter. 'Wait, who are you, behind that mask? You look familiar."

Comrade Bandito looked shocked. "What sorcery is this? A talking ape as a pet?"

A beautiful woman approached. "Don't be ridiculous. It's a lemur. And I'm sure he prefers the term 'companion'."

Pointdexter sighed. "I think I'm in love."

"Comrade Bandito," said the woman. "Put down your rifle."

The masked man reluctantly lowered his weapon.

"Hello," said the woman, shaking their hands. "I'm Isadora. You must be starving. Come. I think the venison stew is finished, but I have some bread and dried apricots."

Comrade Bandito slammed the butt of his rifle on the hard ground. "You're going to give our bread to an enemy?"

"This is no enemy."

Isadora led the pair to her hut.

"Why does Comrade Bandito wear a mask?" asked the lemur.

"He thinks it makes him look more ... fierce."

"Why does he want to look fierce?" he asked.

Isadora served them some dark bread and poured some green wasp honey mead.

"Because he's the leader of the revolution. He has to look intimidating."

"The revolution?" asked The Baron. "Against the king?"

"Of course. What else? We're on our way to storm the castle. It'll be the biggest *coup d'etat* in the history of Moldavia."

"Excellent!" said The Baron, gulping mead. "We'll join you if you will have us."

"It's a long journey," said Isadora. "It will take many moons to get there."

"My lady, you are looking at the very best journeymen you will ever meet. We can walk thousands of miles and hunt and forage for food and cook with flair. We will carry your bags!"

Isadora shrugged. "I don't have any bags."

"Pointdexter here is also very talented at finding fresh water in a desert."

The lemur nodded enthusiastically.

"Hmm," she said, crossing her arms. "Can you fight?"

"Of course we can fight," said Pointdexter. "We once killed a 40-ft croc—"

"We can fight," said The Baron.

Isadora took their empty plates from them. "Then you'll be a welcome addition."

The evening was warm and golden, and the firebugs celebrated by putting on a show for the rebel army. But when the sun went down, the wind came up. It whistled through the holes in the walls, and the room grew blue with cold. Isadora invited the Baron to share her bed, and they lay together, close, like ivory and ebony spoons, while Marcus Pointdexter kept their feet warm.

Over the next few months, the revolutionaries travelled north towards the castle, picking up other volunteers along the way. This included an apple farmer who lost his crop due to King Zam's shortsighted agricultural policies; a father who had seventeen hungry children at home; and a smelly vagrant who had nothing better to do. Some of the men had joined just to be part of something. Some of the men were marching because they wanted to see the legendary Royal Castle and watch it fall. But some of the advancers were true revolutionaries with motives as clear as ice. Their hearts were pumping the violet blood of rebels with a cause.

· · ·

"Can you hear that? Can you hear that?" asked Comrade Bandito. "Stop! Stop, everyone."

Isadora freezes. "It's the royal guard. We're here. We've reached the castle."

The men cheered.

"Holy Moldavia, men, keep it down! We hardly want to announce our arrival."

There was some muttering, and an apology.

"So," said The Baron. "What is your strategy to penetrate the castle's defences?"

Comrade Bandito put his hands on his hips. "We need to gather intelligence first."

One of the rebel soldiers murmured, "Intelligence? Pah!" When Comrade Bandito looked at him sharply, he continued. "We've been travelling for seven seasons. We don't want to mess about, now that we're here. I say we advance. Right now! I say we storm the castle!"

The others mumbled in agreement.

"Listen, men," said Bandito.

Isadora cleared her throat.

"And women," he quickly added.

Marcus Pointdexter cleared his throat.

"And ... primates. The royal castle of the Kingdom of Moldavia is a building unlike any other. One does not simply march up to it and lay siege."

"Aye," said one of the rebels. "It has a deadly maze, to begin with."

"Exactly!" said Bandito.

"And the snapping jaws of the gharials are legendary."

The rebels reluctantly agreed.

"Fine, fine," said the impatient one. "What do you suggest?"

"What we require," said their leader, "is a first arrow."

"A what, now?"

"A courageous man who will go first. An infiltrator. A reconnoitre."

"Someone who will assess the situation," said Isadora. "Perhaps even find a way to allow us access with minimal bloodshed. Someone who will most likely die a violent and painful death."

"Now," said Comrade Bandito, "I'm assuming that due to the danger inherent to the task, there are no volunteers?

"To the contrary!" said The Baron, who stepped forward.

The lemur sighed. "Oh, brother."

"I'd be honoured to be your first arrow," said The Baron. "I will leave immediately!"

"I'll go, too," said Isadora.

"I feel as if I should be the one to go," said Bandito.

"No, Comrade. You are needed here. You need to lead your army when the time is right. We'll send you a signal when the coast is clear."

Bandito thought it over. "All right," he said. "Here, take a sandwich."

The trio walked and crept and eventually crawled in the sweet, soft clover and double-edged thorns until they reached the castle grounds. There was, indeed, a gigantic maze, clipped expertly from hundreds upon hundreds of tall snickerbushes. Once they entered the labyrinth, they were able to stand up again, undetected.

"They say that it can take days to navigate this maze," said The Baron. "That you end up driven mad by the puzzle—or, worse, starving—and forced to eat the poisonous snickerberries."

"That won't happen to us," said Isadora.

"How do you know?" asked Pointdexter.

"I was taught the way."

"What?" asked The Baron. "How?"

"It's a long story."

"I'd love to hear it," he said.

"I'll tell you one day."

While it felt like the trio was walking in circles for hour upon hour, they were indeed making good progress. They were a paltry mile from the exit when they got terribly lost.

"I don't understand it," said Isadora. "I've walked this maze a hundred times. The path is engraved on my heart. I know this is the right way, but it's a dead-end."

"It's simple," said The Baron.

Pointdexter looked up at him. "It is?"

"They've changed it. Not difficult to do. Plant a few new bushes *et voila.*"

"But what will we do? It's getting dark."

"Let's sit down for a moment and rest."

"We don't have time!" she cried.

"We'll have our sandwiches and figure a way out."

The trio sat down and began to eat.

"These sandwiches are awful," said The Baron.

"Oh, I should have warned you. Comrade Bandito makes terrible sandwiches."

The Baron opened his knapsack and pulled out a bundle of golden grass.

"What are you doing?" asked Isadora. "What is that?"

"I've just had an idea."

"Those are blades of golden grass, from Shamrocky," said Marcus Pointdexter.

"They're magnetic, see? So, in theory..."

Happy understanding dawned on Isadora's face. "They should be able to point us north."

So the Baron, Isadora, and Marcus Pointdexter used the magnetic grass as a golden compass to find their way out of the deadly maze. When they emerged on the other side, the sun was setting in the distance, burning the landscape around it like a fiery globe. The air was painted pink and orange, and the Baron was sure that Isadora had never looked more beautiful.

"Isadora—" said The Baron.

"Yes?" She looked at him intently. "Have you got a plan? To evade the ghastly gharials?"

They all looked down at the gharial-infested moat, the creatures savagely snapping their jaws.

"They look especially hungry," said Marcus Pointdexter. "Vicious things. Legend has it that they are 100% lethal."

"Our chances aren't good," said The Baron.

"But you do have a plan?" Isadora asked.

"I do. But ... before we have the chance to capitulate to our watery graves, I ... I need to tell you something."

"And I need to tell YOU something," she said.

The snapping and thrashing of the gharials got louder.

Pointdexter cleared his throat. "Could we perhaps save the heart-to-heart for *after* the attack of the amphibians? The sun has almost set, and I feel we'll have more of a chance while we can still, well, see them."

"Good point. Bravo. Isadora—can you swim?"

"Of course I can."

"All right. Pointdexter, climb into my knapsack, I'll strap it to my back. I'll go in first and fight the crocodilians off. Isadora, you swim in my wake. I'll protect you from the front."

Isadora whips out her pistol.

"And I'll protect you from the back."

She loaded the gun.

"Holy Moldavia!" said The Baron. "That's a handsome pistol. Ivory?"

"You have a good eye, Baron. Let's go."

They entered the perilous water. It was an epic battle between man and beast. The Baron wrestled seventy-six gharials on his way across the water, protected by his nori-leaf suit. Isadora shot the stragglers that wouldn't let go. As they reached the middle of the moat, the Baron lost his strength. He found that he could no longer swim, carry Marcus Pointdexter *and* fight off the infernal creatures.

"It's okay, Baron," said the lemur. "Leave me behind."

"Never!" yelled The Baron.

"It's the only way you'll survive!"

Still, The Baron refused.

Just then, a new wave of gharials swam up to attack them, and the Baron knew, with a sinking heart, that he would not be able to fight them off. Isadora tried to shoot them, but the pistol became jammed. Marcus Pointdexter, realising that the only way to save the Baron was to dive in, executed a most elegant swan-dive into the teeming grey water. But the Baron knew that Pointdexter, despite his bravado, could not swim, so he dived in after him. Once the Baron's nori suit was fully submerged, it turned into a merman tail. Not only was the Baron able to swim with renewed vigour, but the presence of the sparkling mermaid scales completely subdued the gharials. It was as if the crocodilians were mesmerised by the glinting sequins and their fang-filled jaws snapped shut, and stayed shut. The Baron heard the tinkling laugh of the mermaids.

The Baron rescued Pointdexter. They reached the opposite bank and collapsed gratefully on the land. Poor Pointdexter was coughing and spluttering.

"That was incredible," said Isadora, panting. "What—"

With a dangerous whistle, an arrow sheared the air and pierced the tree trunk behind her. She yelled in fright, then tucked and rolled.

"The king's guard," said The Baron. "They've seen us."

Another arrow just missed them, the shaft vibrating in the air next to The Baron's bare feet. Pointdexter gasped.

"Follow me," whispered Isadora. "I know the way to a secret passage."

They sprinted away from the attackers, running around the base of the castle wall while arrows nipped at their heels. Isadora stopped when she found what she was looking for: a small door that blended almost seamlessly into the stone wall. She desperately tried the handle, but it was locked. An arrow missed her head by less than an inch. Isadora swore and kicked the door. "It's locked. And I no longer have the key."

"Stand back," said The Baron, and tried to knock it down with his bulk, but it didn't work. The darkening sky rained arrows all around them.

"It's such a strange door," mused the lemur. "So small! As if it had been built by goblins."

"What did you say?"

"Nothing. Just that it's small, it's like a goblin door."

This gave The Baron an idea. He tore the perfect fish skeleton from the cord around his neck and slotted it into the keyhole. The skeleton key turned smoothly, and the door swung open. They rushed inside and slammed it shut behind them. Out of breath and relieved, they knew they had to keep going.

"This castle is the size of a small independent country," said The Baron. "How will we find the king?"

Isadora wrenched two fire-torches from the wall and lit them, handing one to The Baron. "The king will be in his cigar lounge," she said. " I know the way."

They scampered through the secret passages until they reached a trapdoor in the low ceiling. Isadora handed her weapon to the Baron.

"You go ahead," she said. "I'll get the others."

They nodded at each other, and The Baron touched her cheek before she disappeared back down the passage, towards the gharials and the deadly maze, and Comrade Bandito.

The Baron smashed the trapdoor open and hauled himself up into the lounge with a flourish. King Zam, dressed in opulent gold silks, dropped his cigar in shock.

"What in the name of—"

The Baron pointed Isadora's pistol at him. "King Zam, I take it?"

"King Zam, I am."

"I'm the Baron of Balaclavia. You're the ruthless, reckless King of Moldavia. You starve your people, and you paint your streets with their blood. I wasn't expecting you to be so short."

"I beg your pardon?"

The Baron lifted the ivory-handled gun. "You deny it?"

"Wholeheartedly!"

"Well, then, sir, you are both a rapscallion and a liar!"

"*Your majesty* is my preferred title."

"There is nothing majestic about the starving peasants I have come across, the ruined farms, the high taxes."

"High taxes? Hungry people? Hang on ... now that you mention it, it does sound a little familiar."

"Am I to believe that you know nothing of the absolutely appalling state of your kingdom?"

"Well, I ... ah ... just assumed that if something were wrong, someone would tell me."

"Well, I am here to tell you that this is a revolution. A *coup d'etat*. Consider yourself ... overthrown."

"This is all a bit sudden," said the king. "I don't know what to say."

"You're not going to try to fight?"

"Absolutely not. You're five times the size of me."

"Ah, okay. Good. That's very civilised of you."

The Baron pocketed the firearm.

"Hold on just a moment," said King Zam. "I recognise that. Where did you get that ivory-handled pistol?"

Just then, Isadora levered her body up, out of the trapdoor. She straightened her back and puffed out her chest. "Where do you think he got it, Zam?"

"My queen!" exclaimed Zam, arms open. "My love! My dearest wife! I thought I'd lost you forever!"

Marcus Pointdexter was quite taken aback. "My *queen?*"

"I left you years ago," said Isadora. "I am no longer your queen."

"You'll always be my queen."

The Baron was as puzzled as the lemur. "Isadora ... You wanted us to overthrow your own kingdom? Your own ... husband?"

"I had no choice. It was the only way to get him to listen. We have a duty to protect the people of the kingdom."

"I'm listening now! I'm listening! What needs to change?"

Isadora retrieved a roll of parchment from her pocket and unspooled it. "There are a hundred things on this list. The most pressing being your economic policy on agriculture."

"I'll do it!"

"You will? You don't feel the need to try to hang on to your disgustingly high taxes, only to be ousted in your ridiculous golden silk pyjamas by our rebel army?"

King Zam looked hurt. "I quite like these pyjamas."

"They do bring out your eyes," said The Baron.

"My mother used to say that my eyes were like sapphires," said the king. "Hang on, did you say 'rebel army'?"

They heard yelling and gunshots in the distance.

"They're right outside. They'll be in here any moment. Would you prefer execution by snickerberries, gharials, or your trusty golden guillotine?"

The king threw himself at Isadora's feet. "Help me! Save me! I don't want to die!"

"Sign this document, and you will be spared!"

The lemur handed him a pen, and the king scribbled his signature on the parchment.

"Good. We will start implementing these changes immediately."

The king hugged Isadora and came away, looking shocked.

"Isadora? You have a big belly. Where did that come from? It's not ... You're not ... you can't be —"

"I'm with child."

"It's impossible! I haven't seen you in years! It's some kind of wonder! Some immaculate conception! A miracle! You've always been a magical woman."

"The baby belongs to the Baron. And so do I."

The Baron looked at Isadora in wonder, but the moment was spoilt when King Zam lost his temper.

"The Baron? This baron? You village muck! You Scaramouche! You won't get out of here alive!"

The king launched himself at The Baron and the two men scuffled in the castle hall. There was pushing and punching, gasping and groaning. The King had his emerald-studded scimitar to the Baron's throat, who, in turn, had Isadora's ivory pistol buried in the King's belly.

"I've got you by the balls, now, you scoundrel!"

"Well, technically, you have me by the throat," whispered the Baron. "My balls are located in another place entirely."

The rebel army, having defeated the castle guards, stormed into the room. Comrade Bandito aimed his weapon at the king. "Hands off my brother, King Zam!"

The Baron stared at Bandito as he pulled off his mask. "Dash?"

"Yes, it's me. And you'd better drop that scimitar now, King, or I'll blow you full of holes with this flintlock and feed what's left of you to your scaly beasts."

"Alright, alright," said Zam, lowering his scimitar and taking a few steps backwards.

Dash looked at his soldiers. "Tie him up."

"Be gentle with him," said Isadora.

"We have done it, men," announced Dash. "We have saved the people of the Kingdom of Moldavia!"

The Rebel army cheered, and The Baron swept Isadora up into a long and passionate kiss.

～

A few moons later, we find ourselves in a castle bedroom, decorated by the raven-post the Baron had sent his mother while he had been on his grand adventure. She had brought them with her when she had been summoned and had decorated the prince's nursery with them. They were surrounded by, amongst other things: an adder stone; a whitewood bonsai sapling; a pouch of cumin incense; an abandoned starling's nest with a single speckled egg inside; a hairbrush made of purple pine needles; a fistful of golden pomegranate jewels; a rapid-polished rock; a bunch of lavender; a pretty fossil; an old kidney bean engraved with a heart. In short, they were surrounded by love. Also, on the shelf, was the Baron's favourite childhood book: "The Baron of Balaclavia's Tales of His Fantastic Journeys and Fabulous Adventures."

Isadora is screaming blue murder—

"You can do it, Isadora, you can do it," says the midwife with baseball mitts for hands. "Let's have one more push. Give it all you've got."

The Baron mops the perspiration from his queen's brow. "You have never looked more beautiful."

Isadora strains and screams as she uses all the strength in her body to push. I daresay that you would be screaming too if you were giving birth to an infant as buxom as The Baron's baby.

"His head is out!" shouts the midwife. "One more push, love."

The baby makes his bloody appearance and gives a healthy yell.

"It's a boy!"

"He's beautiful," says Isadora. "Isn't he beautiful? He has his father's handsome chin!"

The midwife nods enthusiastically. "I've never seen a more beautiful baby. And he's a record-breaker, by the looks of it."

"What do you mean?"

"He weighs 68 pebblestone!" She wraps the infant in a soft muslin receiving blanket that had seen dozens of babes before him. The midwife had boiled it in sweet streamwater with dandelion flowers and let it dry in the shade. "He's a big boy, that's for sure."

"Yes. Yes, he is," Isadora and The Baron coo as the midwife hands the baby over. "He's destined for big things."

7

SLASHPURSE

The courtroom was writhing with rabble. All the people in town had come to witness the trial of Suzie Slashpurse: crossdresser, madam, and thief. When Susan strode through the cobbled streets of 17th century London—her pet mastiff at her heels—people would step out of her way. She had glittering eyes and the air of a pirate, smoked like a chimney, and was known as the Queen of Pickpockets. As a girl she'd been a boisterous tomboy, bored by common girls' pursuits, going as far as calling her embroidery sheet a shroud. Suzie preferred boys' company—the rougher, the better. She was a rumpscuttle who could not think quietly and would not be tamed.

When Slashpurse entered the courtroom, it was to an anthem of cheers and hisses. She was wearing her customary men's clothing; all that was missing was her smoking pipe and the curse words that usually shot out of her mouth like stones from a catapult. Most of her loyal friends and supporters were locked outside; they had caused enough trouble leaning into the prosecutor and constable as they had walked into court that day.

The judge smoothed down his whiskers as he watched the accused being led to the stand. The crowd hushed up to listen to the charges being read out by a sonorous-voiced court official.

"Susan Newgate is accused of the theft of a golden pocket watch of which she was caught in possession, it being displayed in the window of her residence in London town."

"I plead not guilty," said Slashpurse, hands bound by steel cuffs. The bawdy onlookers booed and cheered.

The prosecutor wore a dirty wig and a scowl that would make a rabid bitch self-conscious.

"Ms. Newgate," he said. "Is it not true that you were arrested in August 1601 for stealing someone's handbag at Clerkenwell in London? A crime for which you confessed?"

"I was found not guilty," said Slashpurse.

"You confessed to the crime."

"And I was acquitted."

"Two years later you were prosecuted for taking a purse of twenty-five shillings."

Susan Newgate stared at the man as if he had challenged her to a duel right there and then, in the churning courtroom.

"In fact," said the man. "Your uncle, a respected man of the cloth, arranged for you to board a ship to the New World so that you could start a new life for yourself. But you jumped overboard and swam back."

"Where is the crime?" asked Susan. "Besides, my uncle is a frightful man."

"Isn't it true," said the prosecutor, "that you have had your hands burned a total of four times for your grubbing and thievery?"

"I was a lost soul," she said. "But now, I am found."

There are sniggers from the gallery, and Slashpurse fights the pulling up of her own lips.

The prosecutor is not deterred. "Eight years later, at the behest of King James, you were sent to Bridewell Prison for your inappropriate dress."

Slashpurse snorts. "Inappropriate?"

"Women should not dress as men," he said. "It's a rude inclination."

"You'd like to see me in a skirt, then?" she asked, raising an eyebrow in a provocative way. The onlookers slapped their knees and laughed.

"I don't want to see you in trousers," he said. "It's uncomely and indecent."

"Oh, dear," she mused. "I wouldn't want to be perceived as *uncomely*. It just so happens that I don't like to see *you* in trousers, either. Does that mean you'll take them off?"

Whistling and clapping made the prosecutor blush a deep shade of raspberry preserve; he spent a moment recovering.

"Will you please get to the point?" asked Judge Fairfax, pinching the bridge of his nose. He'd had enough of the banter between prosecutor and prisoner. He reached for his water.

"The point is, your honour," said the glowering man, "that Susan Newgate is a highwaywoman and career criminal who will continue to steal unless she is locked up for good. She is a festering boil on the rump of the people."

The judge spat out his water. The guard offered him a handkerchief, but he waved it away. He looked directly at the accused. "What say you, Susan Newgate?"

What could she say? No one had expected Susan Newgate to turn out as she had, with the niftiest fingers in the business. Certainly not her honest parents, of whom she was the sole daughter. Her father had been a humble cobbler who lived near the Barbican at the upper end of Aldersgate Street. Her parents adored her—even though she was hard to handle—but they passed away when she was a child. Suzie had grown into the most famous purse-picker in London, going as far as training other young sneak-thieves how to cut purse strings and snatch bags with minimal interference. For this—and other things—she had a long and loyal following.

"I would be happy to serve the sentence," said Suzie, "if the crime can be proven."

Judge Fairfax seemed to accept this and turned his attention back to the prosecutor, who ground his teeth.

"It came to my attention, Ms. Newgate, that you've been using your home as a brothel and hiring out ladies of ill repute."

"Now, how would you come by this kind of information?" asked Susan.

He ignored her, but she could tell by the second blushing of his cheeks that he had heard the question.

"And if that crime isn't heinous enough," he said—he didn't have proof of her as a whoremistress—"It came to my attention also that you have been displaying stolen items in the front window of your primary residence on Fleet Street."

"Stolen?" asked Newgate. "Nonsense. They were gifts from my friends."

"Your pickpocket friends," said the prosecutor. "In fact, am I correct in saying that you act as a fence in selling the previously mentioned items?"

"Not at all!" scoffed Slashpurse.

"A Mister Gerald Hannam walked past your home the other day and spotted his gold watch in the self-same window. The very gold watch he had been relieved of just days before!"

"Do you have proof of this?" rumbled the judge.

"I do. Mister Hannam immediately called a constable who saw the contents of the window and confiscated the watch, which is now in my pocket."

"How do you know it's Hannam's?" asked the judge.

"It has his initials engraved on the back, your honour. G. C. H. George Christopher Hannam."

The judge crimped his lips and made an impatient gesture to bring him the watch, but when the prosecutor dipped his fingers into his breast pocket, his hand came away empty. He looked confused, then glared furiously at Slashpurse. "You did this," he rasped.

Susan returned his fiery stare and held up her handcuffed wrists, shrugging. In that moment of silence, they could hear the crowd gathered outside; a band of lute-players, prostitutes, and expert pickpockets chanting for Suzie's release.

8

LITTLE SPARROW

*T*his story was originally written as a play and optioned by the national broadcaster, the SABC.

~

The car is almost silent as it moves along the smooth, empty road.

"Are we there yet? Are we there yet?" asks Margaret from the back seat.

Judy laughs.

"Mom," says Andrew, taking his eyes off the road for just long enough to frown at his mother in the rearview mirror. "Please act your age."

"Act my age?" demanded the old woman. "Are you insane?"

"If I am," said Andrew, "then I know who I got it from."

"You will be very pleased to know, my dear," said Margaret, "that dementia is NOT, in fact, contagious."

"Thank God for that."

"And even if it was, you know that I have the fit young brain of a 21-year-old. It's all the Sudoku I do. Are there any more jelly beans?"

"Talking of insanity, Margaret," says Judy, passing the bag of sweets to her mother-in-law. "I still think you are crazy for wanting to live in this place with a bunch of strangers instead of coming to live with us."

"Darling," says Margaret. "When you get to my age, the LAST thing you want is to be coddled by your children. I have no desire whatsoever to play at the role-reversal that comes with moving in with the fruit of my loins. Besides, I crave company."

Judy turns to look at her. "You don't like our company?"

"Of course I do! But you have such busy lives. I want someone to play cards with. Someone to go for walks with. Easy company: that's what I need."

"You can change your mind any time, Ma," says Andrew. "You'll always be welcome."

"There is no way I'll change my mind. Do you know how much I've paid for this place? The deposit was the same amount I spent on my first apartment. And it was non-refundable!"

"But if you do," Andrew says. "There is a room waiting for you at our house. You know that."

"I know you don't want to be a burden," says Judy, "but you won't be!"

"Your father and I made a promise, Andrew—when you were knee-high to a grasshopper—that we would never become 'those' kind of old people."

"What does that mean?" asks Judy. "Who are THOSE kind of old people?"

"Ah, dear heart. You know the ones. Creaking and cracking and moaning and groaning. 'My knees!' they always say, when they get up from a chair, and it sounds like a dog crunching a chicken bone. 'Ooh! Ooh! My knees!' Crunch, crunch, crunch."

Judy laughs.

"And the stories they tell! Oh my God, the stories. You would think that ancient people would have some interesting stories but do they ever tell the good ones?"

"Never!" says Andrew.

"Ha! See? Never! Instead, they bore you to tears with their medical issues. They regale you with every minute detail of their latest surgery. Every stitch. Every physio appointment. And they never call them surgeries, they call them 'ops'. 'You know, I'm going in for an op,' they say. 'Ah, I've just had a little op.' Gah!"

Judy can't help chuckling.

"Stop laughing," says Andrew. "You're encouraging her!"

"... And intimate details about their bowels. Things you can never un-hear! You know, I always want to say, if I wanted to know intimate details about your assho—"

"Language, Mom!"

"If I wanted to know the intimate details about your large intestines I would bloody well ask! Pssh. Anyway. Those are the kinds of mind-numbing old folk that move in with their children and never move out. You can't honestly tell me that THAT is what you want."

"But you're not like that, Margaret. Not at all. We'd love to have you stay. We love your stories—"

Andrew nods. "You DO have some very entertaining stories."

"And you have the knees of a spring chicken!" says Judy.

"Ha!"

There is a pause in the conversation, then Andrew speaks. "A little sparrow."

"Sorry, love?"

"Little Sparrow," says Andrew. "That's what Dad used to call Mom. They were in Paris on their honeymoon, and they fell in love with Edith Piaf."

"Ah," says Judy, smiling. "Then the knees of a little sparrow!"

There is another thoughtful pause.

"Maybe," says Margaret, "when you see this place you'll understand. It's like Club Med! There's a heated pool and a rec centre and a cocktail bar and everything. They have 24-hour room service!"

Andrew guffaws. "A cocktail bar? At a nursing home? What's next? Happy Hour?"

"It's not a 'nursing home,' Andrew, dear. It's a 'Retirement Destination.'"

"A *what?*"

"It's all about marketing, you see? Kids don't feel half as bad sending their decrepit parents off to a 'holiday club'."

"Still. A cocktail bar?"

"Judy, do you see now why I can't live with you two? I'm 86 bloody years old—"

"Language!" scolds Andrew.

"As I was saying, I'm 86 BLOODY years old, and if I want to spend the days swearing and drinking Pimm's and playing bloody strip poker, then I will do it WITHOUT the disapproving glare from the very boy whose bare bottom I used to smack for stealing my menthol cigarettes."

"That does sound quite lovely, Marge. If Andrew gets too strict with me, I shall come and spend a few days with you. We can drink cocktails together. Although I'm not sure about the strip poker ..."

Margaret pats Judy on the shoulder. "We all have our boundaries, dear."

"Some fewer than others," Andrew murmurs.

A woman in a red suit and matching lipstick rushes to greet them. "Welcome! Welcome! The Meads, I presume? I'm the club coordinator at 'The Rambling Rose'. I'm Bernadette, but everyone calls me 'Bee'."

"We know," says Margaret.

"You know? How clever!" She raises her voice when she speaks directly to Marge. "Been doing our homework, have we?"

"No, it's emblazoned on that huge badge on your blouse."

"Ha! Of course! I've been wearing it for so long now that I don't even see it anymore! Almost 30 years now!"

"You must have started when you were 12," says Andrew.

"Ah, Mr. Mead, you are too kind. Too kind. But I'm afraid I'm a lot older than you give me credit for."

"I'd say a hundred, in the shade," murmurs Margaret.

Andrew elbowed his mother in the ribs. "Mom!"

"Oh, give me a break. I was kidding! I'm on a sugar high from eating too many of those jelly beans, and I'm just excited to be here. If I weren't wearing my adult diaper, I'd be peeing all over this pretty floor."

Bernadette looks shocked.

"Please forgive my mother's inappropriate sense of humour. She is neither incontinent, nor does she wear diapers. She's just, well, she's an imp. That's what she is."

Margaret pretends to be shocked. "Well, I never."

"It's true, Mom, you're an imp."

"You know, you try to raise your kids to respect their elders, and this is what you get."

"Come on, you two, cut it out," says Judy, but she does look amused.

"Twelve long hours in labour, eighteen long years of childhood. Then what? First, they insult you. Then they ship you off to some nursing home to wither and die."

Bernadette smiles brightly. "We prefer the term 'Retirement Destination'."

Margaret guffaws. "I bet you do!"

"Okay, that's enough for now," says Judy. "You've made a sterling first impression. I'm sure Bee would like to show us around."

Bernadette rings a small service bell, and a porter appears. "Ah, there you are. John, please fetch Mrs. Mead's things from the car. She'll be staying in room 32."

"Bet you the previous tenant just pegged," whispers Margaret to Judy. "Hope they changed the sheets."

After the tour of the premises, they sit on the restaurant patio. Elton John is on the sound system and is updated only by the clinking of ice in their highball glasses.

"So, what do you think, Marge? Now that you've seen the place properly and unpacked your things?"

"They pour their gins a bit shy," says Margaret, looking into her empty glass. "But apart from that, I think it's good."

"Just 'good'?" says Andrew. "This place is a veritable 5-star resort. We're going to start bringing the kids here for holidays."

"It's good. Of course it's good. You know what your father always used to say about me: I have great taste."

"Did you see the spread for dinner?" asks Andrew. "Incredible."

"I told you it was like Club Med. Now do you see why I'd rather be here than eating Judy's chicken casserole every Thursday night?"

Judy looks offended. "I thought you liked chicken casserole! I make it especially for you!"

"Ah, dear. I do love you. But the chicken is already dead when you buy it, you know. There is no cause to murder it further in your kitchen."

"I know what you're doing, Mom," says Andrew.

"You do? Good! That makes one of us."

"You're trying to make us cross with you so that we feel better about leaving you here. Like when you shout at a dog and throw a stone to get it to run away from you because you know it's for its own good."

"I am doing no such thing," insists Marge. "This is just my regular—sparkling!—personality!"

Andrew and Judy finish their drinks and set the dripping glasses on the table. Judy looks at Margaret in a tender way. "You'll be okay here, on your own?"

"I'm hardly on my own, dear. There are hundreds of people here. I'll certainly have the company that I wanted."

Andrew looks around. "I wouldn't say 'hundreds'."

"Really? I'd say it's rather quite crowded."

"Okay," says Judy, standing up. "I'd love to stay for another, but we'd better get a move on if we have any hope of getting home in the light. We'll come to visit you really soon."

They hug, and Judy tosses Margaret another packet of sweets.

"Waiter?" says Marge. "Waiter? I'll have another gin and tonic, please. And this time, make it a double."

A few days later, Margaret is in her room, drinking sherry and watching a game of cricket. South Africa is bowling, and they get a wicket.

"Bowled! Yes! Howzat! He's out! Great ball."

Without warning, the channel changes to a nature programme.

"What the blazes?" says Margaret. "Where is that remote?"

She changes it back to cricket, but within five minutes it hops back to the wildlife show.

"Damn it. What is going on?" She changes it back to the sports channel and waits for a few minutes, remote in hand, for the television to glitch again. It stays on the cricket, so she lays the remote down and picks up her sherry.

"That's better. Come on, Proteas. You can do it! Just a few more balls to go."

The next time it changes, Margaret slams down her drink and stands up. She picks up the phone.

"Hello? John? It's Marge. Marge. Yes, Mrs. Mead. In room 32. There's something wrong with my television. It keeps changing channels, and I'm missing the match."

"Is it an emergency?" asks John.

"Yes, it is! We're in the final few overs, and they still have three more batsmen to come in!"

"I'll be there as soon as I can."

"Hurry! They're hitting sixes all over the show!"

The next time it changes over to the nature documentary, the door opens.

"Is that you, John?" asks Margaret. "Thank goodness! That was quick. I was just ... hello? Who's there?" Margaret keeps quiet for a moment, then, startled, drops the remote. "Oh no, not you again! Get out! Do you hear me? Get out!"

"Boys, take that ball outside. I'm not asking again!" yells Judy. Her hair is sticking up in all directions, and her cheeks are flushed from the heat of the oven. One of the boys runs up and grabs a handful of grated cheese. Judy smacks his hand.

"Ow!"

"I warned you! Now, outside, both of you."

The boys tumble into the front garden just as their father arrives home from work. The children yell their greetings, and Andrew comes in, chuckling. "Hello, beautiful."

"Beautiful?" asks Judy, pushing a damp strand of hair out of her eyes. "Really?"

"You're always beautiful when you cook."

"So that's not very often, then."

They kiss, and Andrew's eyebrows shoot up. "Smells good."

Judy snaps the tea towel at him. "Don't act so surprised!"

Andrew opens a bottle of wine and pours them each a glass. "So, I spoke to Mom's doctor today."

"Since when does Marge have a doctor?" asks Judy.

"Since Busy Bee decided she needed one, apparently. Mom, of course, disagrees."

"Of course she does! That woman's never been sick a day in her life. That's what? A hundred and twenty years?"

"Close. She's 86. That's what she says, anyway."

"86! She is a marvel. She really is."

"I'm sure that she's going to reach 100 despite her hedonistic ways. Anyway, it's not that kind of doctor."

"No?" says Judy. "What kind of doctor then? Don't tell me she's going to have her face done. That place really IS like a luxury getaway. I wouldn't be surprised if they offered nips and tucks along with their five-course dinners."

Andrew doesn't laugh, so Judy stops stirring the sauce and looks at him.

"A ... psychologist," he says.

Judy switches off the stove and picks up her glass of wine, holding it against her chest. "A psychologist? I'm listening."

"It's nothing serious," he says.

"It doesn't sound like it's nothing serious."

"He—Dr Mhlekwa, lovely chap—wanted her history. There's nothing in her file."

"There's nothing in her file because she's as healthy as a horse," says Judy.

"She's been acting ... strangely."

"She has always acted strangely. They're probably just not used to having such energetic octogenarians around. What happened? Did they catch her tanning in the nip? Or skinny-dipping?"

117

"She's been complaining about a woman ... in her room."

"But she has a private room."

"They are all private rooms. But apparently, she keeps finding this woman going through her things."

"So, where does the psychologist come in?"

"Well, she tried to get the lady to leave. There was a scuffle. A nurse came in and found Mom sitting on the floor, surrounded by all her clothes and make-up. Disorientated. Pearls all over the floor."

"Pearls?"

"Her pearl necklace had been broken. The one my Dad gave her in Paris. She was distraught."

"I'd also be upset! Poor thing! Where was the awful woman?"

"She had fled the scene. Why are you smiling?"

Judy tries to hide her sudden urge to laugh by dishing up dinner.

"I'm sorry," she says. "It's just the picture in my head of an ancient woman fleeing ... one painful step at a time with her walker. Clutching one of Marge's designer scarves and a bag of sweets."

Andrew pretends to be cross. "Don't be ridiculous, Jude."

"I'm sorry," she says, wiping her eyes.

"No one can flee with a walker. She must have had one of those scooters."

They look at each other and swallow their laughter.

. . .

Over dinner, Andrew puts down his cutlery. "I know it's far," he says, "but I want to go and see her. Just to make sure she's okay."

"Of course! I'll come along. Let's make a weekend of it. The boys can go to the Jacksons. We can find a little B&B nearby and spend some proper time with her. Not have to rush back."

"By 'some proper time' I presume you mean Happy Hour?"

"You know me so well."

When Andrew and Judy arrive at The Rambling Rose retirement destination, they find Margaret sitting on her own at the pool.

"Hi, kids!" she yells. She waves enthusiastically, as if she's in a crowd of people and needs to get their attention. Her bracelets click and jangle.

"Oh my," says Judy, under her breath. "Is that a *gold* bikini she's wearing?"

"I think it's leopard print."

"Leopard print with ... gold sequins."

"Hi, Mom!" says Andrew. "Nice tan."

"Ha! Thanks. It's tan-in-a-can," she says, grinning at them. "They have a great salon here."

"And you've had your hair done," says Judy. "It looks lovely."

"I do feel good. But that might be the gin speaking."

"Mom, it's barely past 10 AM!"

119

"Oh, relax Andy, I'm only pulling your leg. I'm as sober as a judge."

"Gin or no gin, you are looking very well," says Judy.

Andrew nods. "You don't look a day over ninety."

"Ninety is the new sixty," says Margaret, flapping her arms. "Give or take a couple of batwings and swollen knuckles."

Judy recoils. "But Marge! Your arm!"

"Oh, it's nothing. I bruise so easily nowadays."

Andrew frowns. "Let's see?"

"It's nothing! Just a little bruise."

"That is not a LITTLE bruise," says Judy.

"It was that terrible woman! But I'm okay now. Really. I told you, you didn't have to come!"

"We wanted to come," says Judy. "We miss you. The chicken casserole misses you."

Margaret giggled.

"I just came to get away from the city. And from Judy's cooking."

A cheerful bell jingles in the distance.

"Ooh, goodie," says Margaret, rubbing her hands together. "Tea-time. They have the most talented pastry chef here. You must try the scones. Best scones I've tasted in ninety-six years! Puts the chef at Claridge's to shame!"

"Hang on, aren't you 86?" asks Andrew.

"Hee! Dear Andy, you're so easy to kid. Too easy. So adorably gullible. Where did I go wrong?"

"He's just a bit on edge. He's worried about you, Marge."

"Pssh. It's just a small bruise. Besides, Andrew has been on edge since he was born. You've never seen a more serious baby. I'm telling you. People used to stop and stare."

"Have you seen that crazy woman again?"

"Rebecca? Yes."

"Yes, you saw her again? Do you know her name? Did you call a nurse?"

"She was in my room last night. She told me her name was Rebecca and that I was in HER room. I rang the bell."

Andrew looks hopeful. "So they caught her?"

"She was very cross with me. Started throwing my things around. Then vanished into thin air before the nurse arrived."

"This must stop," says Andrew. "This is unacceptable."

Judy's mouth hangs open. "She was cross with YOU? The cheek!"

"Look, you two. Calm down. The woman is clearly a bit, well—"

"Unstable!" exclaims Andrew.

"Upset," says Margaret.

Judy's mouth is still open. "Did she hurt you again?"

"No, no, I gave her a wide berth this time. I let her throw her

121

toys, so to speak. She's harmless, really."

"That injury on your arm says otherwise!"

"Oh, forget about my arm, for heaven's sake. I won't have you molly-coddling me."

"I just think they need to identify this person and keep her from causing havoc," says Andrew, and Judy nods. "It's only right."

"They got me to look at mug-shots," says Margaret.

"Mug-shots?" says Judy.

"You know, headshots. It's part of the application process—you need to supply a photograph of yourself so that the staff can learn your name before you arrive."

"And you couldn't find her?" asks Andrew.

"To be honest, dear, I got so bored I only got through half of the pile."

Andrew rubs his temples. "So you didn't finish?"

Margaret gestures at her tan and freshly painted toenails. "I had a salon appointment!"

Andrew sighs. "What are we going to do with you?"

"In more exciting news," says Margaret. "I've met someone!"

"I knew it!" says Judy.

"What do you mean, you knew it? She's barely been here a week!"

"The new hair, the tan, the sparkle in her eyes ..."

"What do you mean, you've met someone?" asks Andrew.

"What do you mean, what do I mean? Do I need to go into detail?"

"No!" he practically shouts. "No details required."

"He's a lovely man—old-world charm and manners. You'll meet him tonight, at dinner. Bordin is his name. Robert. Wonderful chap, and not bad looking either!" She looks at Judy and drops to a whisper. "We've already made it to third base!"

Andrew pretends to block his ears. "This is supposed to be an old age home, not a dating pool!"

"Dearheart, when you get to my age, every game of Bingo is a dating opportunity."

After tea-time, when the sun gets too hot, they decide to go to Margaret's room. What they see when they enter makes Judy gasp. "Margaret!"

"What," says Andrew, "what happened here?"

Margaret's eyes narrow, and she puts her hands on her hips. "Damn that infernal woman!"

"Rebecca did this?"

"Of course she did this!" says Margaret, a slight wobble in her voice. "Who else would have done it?"

"This is ridiculous!" says Andrew. "It has to stop. I'm going to speak to management."

Andrew storms off and Margaret begins to look through the things strewn on the floor. "The necklace. The pearls. I had them in a small box. I need to find it."

Judy drops to her knees. "I'll help you."

"It's no use," says Margaret. "It's gone!"

Judy isn't accustomed to seeing Margaret upset. "We'll find it, don't worry."

"No, we won't. She's taken it!"

"We don't know that."

"I know it. She said the pearls were hers. She was cross with me for wearing them. She lunged for them. That's how the necklace broke. Now it's gone."

There is a heated conversation taking place in the manager's office.

"I won't stand for this!" says Andrew. "Who bullies an 86-year-old woman?"

"Please, Mr. Mead, calm down. Have a seat," says Bernadette. "We need to discuss this in a calm and rational manner."

"Calm down? My mother is being victimised, and you haven't done a thing to stop it!"

"You have the right to be upset, but I don't think you understand the situation."

"What is there to understand?" he demands. "You have a rogue madwoman going through your other resident's things! Attacking them!"

"No," says Bernadette.

"Rebecca! My mother said her name is Rebecca."

"No one has been 'attacked'."

"Have you seen the bruise on my mother's arm?"

"I have. It is unfortunate."

"'Unfortunate'?" says Andrew, gesturing wildly. "My God."

"There is no resident here by the name of Rebecca."

"What are you saying? Is it someone off the street? That's even worse!"

"I've called Dr. Mhlekwa. He'll be here in a moment."

"Unless that doctor tells me that you have this person in hand, I don't see how his presence will help our discussion."

"Please," says Bernadette. "Sit? We have something to show you."

There is a light knock on the door. Bernadette sighs in relief and lets the psychologist in. "Doctor," she says. "Thank you for coming. This is Andrew Mead, you spoke on the phone."

"Of course, good morning, Mr. Mead."

"It hasn't been very good, I can assure you."

"My apologies," says Dr. Mhlekwa. "It was a poor choice of words." He sets up his laptop on his desk. "Now, you may find this upsetting."

"I don't understand—"

"We can talk after the video," says the doctor, and clicks 'play'.

The video is of Margaret Mead's private room. Clothes and

objects are being thrown around the room, and she is shouting and pleading. Her necklace breaks and the pearls scatter all over the floor. Despite her struggling, she is alone.

Andrew watches it twice and then drops his face into his hands. "Oh my God."

"I'm sorry," says Dr. Mhlekwa. "I know this must be very difficult for you."

Andrew is speechless.

"You've had a shock, Mr. Mead. Please, take your time."

"I just ... I don't understand."

"Now, let us not panic," says the psychologist. "One delusional episode does not mean—"

"But it wasn't just one episode, was it? It's been three times now. But I still don't understand. She was 100% *compos mentis* a week ago—before she came here! What have you done to her?"

"There is no way to know that for sure."

"She had a clean bill of health, and you know it! And tell me this: if there was no-one else in the room when she had these 'episodes,' then how did she get that bruise on her arm?"

"She fell back against the dresser when she broke the necklace. Watch here—"

"No, no," Andrew shakes his head. "I don't want to watch it again."

Doctor Mhlekwa clears his throat. "There are steps we can take."

"Steps?"

"To ensure she doesn't hurt herself," says Bernadette. "Or anyone else."

"I'm sorry, I'm still trying to ... process this. What could have caused it?"

"Dementia becomes common at a certain age," says the doctor. "Especially in women."

"Dementia?"

"We can watch her closely, monitor her behaviour. We will only intervene if we have to."

"It's a good thing she is here with us, Mr. Mead," says Bernadette. "We'll be able to take good care of her. The residents agree to round-the-clock supervision when they sign their application."

"You mean, this? Cameras in their rooms?"

"Yes, it's for their safety. The reason we pulled this footage was to identify the interloper in her room."

"Margaret gave us no other indication that she was in distress," says Dr. Mhlekwa. "There is another video clip from this morning."

"I don't want to see it," Andrew says.

"She takes a small box—it looks like a cigar box of sorts—and she hides it under her mattress."

Andrew walks stiffly back to his mother's room and stops at the doorway when he gets there.

"Love!" says Judy, just packing away the last of the clothes that had been on the floor. "You were gone for ages. Are you okay?"

Margaret is sitting in a chair, looking fragile. Her mascara has run down her cheeks. "Did they find her? The woman? I'd like to have a word with her."

"Mom," says Andrew gently. "What's under the mattress?"

"Under the mattress?" she says. "What do you mean?"

"Do you mind if I look?"

"What are you on about?" says Judy. "What does the mattress have to do with anything?"

Andrew lifts the mattress and finds the box of pearls.

"My pearls!" exclaims Margaret.

Judy frowns. "How did you know they were there?"

"Mom," says Andrew in a quiet voice. "Do you remember putting them here?"

Margaret shakes her head. "No, it was the lady. Rebecca. She took them."

"She didn't take them."

Margaret stops. "Oh. Of course."

"What's going on?" asks Judy.

"*You* must have put them here, Mom."

"Yes," says Margaret uncertainly. "Yes, I must have. I must have hidden them from her."

"You don't remember?" asks Judy.

"Now that Andy is saying so, I ... I think I remember doing it."

"Mom, there is no Rebecca. No strange lady is visiting your room."

Margaret's body stiffens. "What are you saying? Of course there is! She keeps harassing me!"

"Please, Andy, you're upsetting her!"

"Let's ... let's talk outside," he says to Judy.

Margaret marches up to her son. "You will NOT talk outside. I will not be discussed as if I am a child! Talk to me! Tell me what is going on!"

"Mom, please. They showed me a video. There is no Rebecca. There is no other woman."

Judy freezes. "What?"

"There was!" shouts Margaret. "She was right here! She's got this long grey hair, and she's always wearing the same stinking yellow dress! She keeps looking through my things and getting angry with me for sleeping in her bed!"

Andrew's face crumples. "Oh, Mom."

"I know! I know what you're thinking. That I've gone mad. But I haven't! She was here. She was as real as you two are now."

Andrew sits down and steeples his fingers. He takes a deep breath.

"Mom. Is it happening again?"

Margaret wipes her melted mascara away. "Is what happening again?"

"The ... visions?"

"Andy!" says Judy. "You told me that Marge has no psychological history."

"That's because I don't!" shouts Margaret.

"You know what I'm talking about, Mom."

"You mean the sparrows?"

"Yes," says Andrew. "I mean the sparrows."

"They were not 'visions'—they were real, and you know it! You saw them!"

Judy crosses her arms. "Will someone please tell me what is going on?"

"After Dad died," says Andrew. "There were—"

"He sent me little sparrows. He kept on sending me sparrows. You know, Edith Piaf? The Little Sparrow? Paris? The little birds would pop up everywhere. He was trying to tell me something."

"That was what you *thought*. That was why we were worried about you."

Margaret ignores her son and turns to Judy. "So many little creatures. They were beautiful, really."

"That is spooky," says Judy. " And romantic."

"It became macabre," says Andrew, pulling his face as if there were a bad smell in the room. "Sparrows don't live forever. We used to find their tiny carcasses everywhere. It became ... sinister."

"Hogwash!" says Margaret. "There wasn't anything sinister about it. They were beautiful, not spooky. They only died because, well, sparrows are just dumb creatures that fly into windows. They can't help it. He stopped sending them once I finally got the message."

"What was the message?"

"That he missed me. Loved me. That he was still there, somewhere. That death is not the end."

Andrew and Judy are awoken from a deep sleep by a phone ringing.

"What time is it?" asks Andrew.

"Midnight," says Judy.

Andrew answers the call.

"Mr. Mead," says Bernadette's urgent voice. "You need to come immediately."

Andrew jolts upright in the strange bed. "What's happened? Tell me what's happened. Is she okay?"

"There's been an accident. Please get here as soon as you can. Come to the hospital wing."

"Mom!" exclaims Andrew. "What happened?"

His mother lies in a hospital bed, clearly disoriented, and in pain.

"Marge!" says Judy, taking her hand.

"Thank God you're here. I want to go home. I don't want to be here anymore. Please take me home."

"Of course," says Andrew. "We'll go right now."

"I'm sorry, that's not possible," says Bernadette.

"Of course it's damn well possible. She is my mother, and I will take her—"

"Her hip," says Bernadette. "It's fractured. She's going to need surgery."

"It's these people," says Margaret. "There are just too many people here. I just get pushed and pulled in all directions."

"How did you fall?" asks Andrew.

"I didn't 'fall'! I didn't 'fall'!"

"Did the woman come back, Margaret?" asks Judy.

Andrew grits his teeth. "Don't start that again!"

"Did she push you, Marge?"

"Judy! That's enough!"

"She pushed me out of my bed. I was sleeping, and she came and just pushed me onto the floor. Said I had to get out of her bed."

Bernadette looks worried. "I think I should call Dr Mhlekwa."

"There are just too many people here. I thought it would be a quiet, peaceful place. They keep touching me, pulling at me."

"We gave her painkillers and a sedative. She was agitated."

"I saw her photo, on the wall," says Margaret.

"The photo of Rebecca?"

"Will you please—" says Andrew, his fury lighting up his face.

"Stop telling me what to say!" says Judy. "I believe her!"

"You 'believe' her? There's nothing to 'believe'! She's delusional!"

"Please," whispers Bernadette. "Let's not upset her further."

"I believe that she believes what she saw."

"What the hell kind of thing is that to say? My mother is lying here with a smashed up face and a broken hip, and you're talking about believing in fairies!"

"Exactly, Andrew! It's your MOTHER. Not some crazy old lady. YOUR MOTHER! And she is trying to tell us something!"

"Shall we go and talk in my office?" asks Bernadette.

"No! Don't leave me. Don't leave me here with all these people."

"We'll stay, Marge," says Judy. "We're here."

"The photo in the corridor. She's there."

"And who are the other people, Marge? Who are all these people grabbing you?"

"They live here. They just want to talk, but they get pushy."

"What do they want to talk about?"

"The usual. Their families. Their kids. They always want me to send messages to their families."

"Messages?"

"As if they don't know how to use a phone."

Margaret passes out.

"Mom? Mom?"

"Let her sleep," says Bernadette. "They'll be taking her into surgery now."

Judy turns to leave.

Andrew's still cross with her. "Where are you going?"

"Where do you think? I'm going to look at the photos in the corridor."

"Let's all go together," says Bernadette. "We can go to my office. I'll order some tea."

Andrew stands aside for the women to walk ahead of him. "We may need something stronger."

Bernadette takes them to the passage with the framed photographs.

Judy stops to study them. "What are all these pictures?"

"We have regular functions," says Judy. "Black tie, poker nights, 60s parties. The porter, John, doubles as a waiter and a photographer. He has a good eye."

"So these are all current residents?"

"No. We keep the most recent photos near the reception and the restaurants. They remind the clients of good times. It keeps the morale up. These particular ones are quite old now—they get relegated further and further away from the main areas."

"So these people here are—"

"Previous residents," says Bernadette. "Yes."

"In other words—" says Andrew.

"They have passed away. Most of them, anyway. Some are excessively good at staying alive."

"This one," says Judy. "This lady. Who is she?"

"Er," says Bernadette. "Let me put my specs on."

She fiddles for the glasses that hang around her neck and puts them on.

"Look, Andrew," says Judy. "Long grey hair. Yellow dress."

"She's wearing pearls," says Andrew.

"Ah," says Bernadette. "That's Mrs. Cawood."

The lights above them flicker.

"That's her," says Judy. "That's the lady Marge described."

"Well, that can't be. Mrs. Cawood passed away years ago."

"Perhaps my mother saw this photo before," says Andrew, searching for a possible explanation. "And somehow this woman became part of her delusions."

"She couldn't have," says Bernadette. "Mrs. Mead's never been in this corridor. It's strictly for hospital patients only."

"Well, there's clearly another explanation. A photo of her some-where else in the building."

Judy shivers. "I think I'd like to see that video now."

. . .

They sit down in Bernadette's office. It's quiet. She opens her desk drawer and takes out a bottle. "Will Scotch suffice?"

"You're a saint. Thank you."

She pours three generous glasses and hands them out, then Judy clicks 'play'.

Judy watches with a shocked expression as Margaret struggles alone in her room.

"I need to see it again."

"Jude, don't do this to yourself," says Andrew.

Judy reaches past her husband and clicks 'play'. They watch the disturbing clip until Judy gasps. "There!" she says. "There!"

"I know," says Andrew. "It's shocking to see her—"

"Look! Look, as the necklace breaks. Just before she falls backwards."

The lights in the office flicker.

"What?" asks Andrew. "What am I looking at?"

"In the dresser's mirror!"

It's Bernadette's turn to gasp. "What was that? What WAS that?"

"It's nothing," says Andrew. "It's a trick of the light."

Judy's shaking. "You can say what you like, but there is a face in that mirror, and it's not Margaret's."

. . .

Three whiskies down, they get an early-morning call that Mrs. Mead is out of surgery. When she wakes up, Andrew is holding her hand.

"Where am I?" Margaret croaks.

"You're in the hospital wing, Marge. At The Rambling Rose."

"We'll take you home as soon as you've been discharged," says Andrew. "They want to keep you for a few days—until you're stronger."

"The Rambling bloody Rose," Margaret says, her voice weak. Judy lifts a glass of water with a straw, and Margaret takes a sip. "Rebecca was here."

There's an uncomfortable silence.

"Was she?" asks Judy.

"She came to apologise."

"Apologise?" splutters Andrew. "For almost killing you?"

"Did she almost kill me?" asks Margaret with a playful look on her face. "What a catastrophe! I didn't realise. I thought I'd just taken a spill."

"Marge," says Judy. "We've got something to tell you."

The patient perks up. "Really?"

"Now, it's quite shocking," says Andrew. "So, if you're not feeling up to it, we can talk about it later."

"How exciting," says Margaret. "You found Rebecca!"

"Yes, we found Rebecca. Also known as Mrs. Cawood, who used to stay in your room. Before she—"

"Before she cashed in her chips," says Margaret.

"You knew?" asks Andrew. "You knew she was ... dead?"

"Of course I *didn't know*. If I had known I wouldn't be in this hospital bed! If I had known that it was a bloody *ghost* that was wrecking my room, I would have hightailed it out of this loony bin and be bunking at your place!"

The married couple stare at Margaret.

"Rebecca came to apologise," she says. "I explained that it was my bed now, not hers, and she kind of had a ... a moment. She didn't know, you see?"

Andrew frowns. "She didn't know it was your bed?"

"She didn't know that she was dead! It was all a bit sudden. One day she was drinking piña coladas and playing bowls and the next day, wham! Massive stroke! That's why her eyes look a bit squinty, see? Then all of a sudden, a strange lady is sleeping in her bed, filling her cupboards, wearing her pearls."

"To her, *you* were the strange lady," says Judy. "You were haunting HER."

"Exactly. But now that she knows what happened, she won't be bothering me any more."

"Mom. Don't say what I think you're going to say."

"I'm going to stay here!"

"No!" says Andrew.

"Marge," says Judy. "You can't!"

"I can, and I will! You see ... the whole crowded thing ... It's because there are hundreds of spirits here."

"You can't be serious," says Andrew.

"Deadly serious. Do you know how many people die in 'retirement destinations'?"

Andrew looks at the ceiling in exasperation. "I can't believe we're having this conversation."

"Hundreds. Literally. Places like this have a VERY impressive fatality rate."

"They need you," says Judy. "To tell them what happened. To send them on their way."

"Exactly!" says Margaret. "Otherwise they're stuck here forever, stumbling about, clogging up the dinner queue, pushing people out of their beds."

"Even if that were true," says Andrew. "Why does it have to be *you?*"

"I'm the only one who can see them! I can put their minds at rest. I think it's wonderful. I've got cult status around here now, you know. Besides, I've grown quite fond of them. There's Sally, who keeps painting landscapes all over the walls. And Helen, who plays the piano beautifully. Barry is a bit of a pain. He keeps changing the channel on my telly to nature documentaries. I miss all the cricket highlights! But they're good company, really. Or will be, until I let them know that they don't belong here anymore. The only thing I regret—"

"Yes?" says Judy.

"Is my beau. I thought we had something. And now—"

"Oh no," says Judy. "Your new boyfriend was a phantom, too?"

"I'm assuming so. I mean, he stood us up for dinner last night, didn't he? Margaret sighs. "And I thought we had such ... chemistry."

"What a shame," says Judy. "Sorry, Marge."

"Ah, well, I'd probably be too busy for a love life anyway, with my new job. Being the resident ghost whisperer and all."

"One step at a time, Mom, we need to get you out of this hospital bed before you start taking over the spirit world."

"Yes! The nurse told me there's no Happy Hour in the hospital wing! It's a travesty. I'm going to get out of here as soon as humanly possible."

Someone arrives at the doorway, and they all look up.

"Ah," says Andrew. "Saint Bernadette!"

"Good morning! How are we feeling today?"

"Alive and kicking," says Margaret with a sparkle in her eye. "Which is more than I can say for most of the people in this room!"

"Er—" says Bernadette, looking spooked. "Do you mean—"

Margaret chuckles. "I'm kidding. It's just us three."

"Not for long," says Bernadette.

"What now?"

"You have a visitor!"

A handsome man with silver hair hobbles into the room, holding flowers. "I heard you took a tumble last night, dear, are you all right?"

Margaret is delighted. "Robert! You're alive!"

"You look quite well, too."

"I mean, I thought you might be ... well, you look positively vital. I can practically hear your pulse from here."

"Those roses are beautiful," says Judy, taking the bouquet. "I'll put them in some water. I'm Judy, and this is Andrew."

"Ah, I've heard all about you. I was terribly sorry to miss dinner last night. I had an urgent errand to attend to." He fishes in his pocket and brings out a bag of sweets.

"Jelly beans!" says Margaret.

Robert smiles. "I know the way to a girl's heart!" He searches in his other pocket. "And this ... is why I missed dinner." He brings out a jewellery box and opens it, revealing Margaret's pearls, which he had re-strung. She smiles warmly at him as he fastens them around her neck. "Thank you."

She moves slightly and winces, then rings the button for the nurse.

"Are you okay?" asks Judy.

"Never better," says Margaret, winking at Judy. "I feel more alive than I have in years. I think it's the company that does it."

The nurse arrives, slightly worried, and out of breath.

"Nurse?" says Margaret. "Nurse? Bring a round of gin & tonics, please. And make mine a double."

∼

9

THE FAMILY ROMANCE OF NEUROTICS

J unichuro Matsumato is a handsome 42-year-old man: dark-haired, wealthy, and devastated. He stares forlornly at the small glass buddha statue illuminated by the blue LED light behind it. There are thousands of the buddhas behind the glowing panes of glass, five hundred per wall. For easy identification, the light behind his wife's buddha glows a different hue as he swipes his card to enter. He doesn't need to be shown where his wife's glass box is. Junichuro visits here every day and has done for 21 months. He never cries.

The bright LEDs glow different colours and gradients according to the season. Junichuro's favourite time to visit is in Autumn when the room is alight with deep oranges and reds. At the moment it's brilliant blue, and he knows if he stands there for long enough, he might see a shooting star. Nishi's star.

Nishi's buddha block is highlighted yellow, which makes Junichuro remember her favourite flowers—tulips. Scented smoke wisps the air. It floats up from the balls of incense burning slowly over the warmed pebbles behind him. There is a button you can press on the glass pane that will play holograms for you: photos and videos of your loved one can dance before you as you sit on the stylish bench provided. But Junichuro doesn't want to watch those today. He knows by heart her every pixel, and his memories are warmer in his head than in the high-tech hologram. Junichuro doesn't sit on the bench or sing a song as he sometimes does. Today is an important day, and he has somewhere to be. It's the last time he'll be visiting his wife's grave.

Junichuro's wife had been a practical woman, but she had also believed in the afterlife. The futuristic charnel house in a temple in downtown Tokyo had been the perfect solution for her burial as it required no maintenance—better than a tomb-stone—and she said she'd enjoy the company of the others. Nishi Matsumato had been lonely in life and didn't want to be lonely when she passed.

Junichuro glances down at his access card; the microchipped plastic is all he has left of his wife, and it isn't enough for him. As he steps out of the elevator on the ground floor, a young man in a smart suit approaches him.

"Ohayō Misutā Matsumato," he says, bowing. "I believe you want to hand in your key card."

Junichuro nods.

"Are you certain?"

"I am."

He had selected and paid for the glass box next to his wife's.

The next time I come here, I won't need a card to get in. I'll be a box of ash.

He passes it to the man. With a sleight of hand, the charnel

144

access card turns into a white business card. Junichuro's forehead creases. "What's this?"

"Forgive my boldness, Sir," says the man. "But I think they may be able to help you."

Junichuro looks at the new card in his hand.

THE FAMILY ROMANCE OF NEUROTICS. There is a phone number on the back.

Junichuro catches the speed train back to his house. He doesn't call it "home" anymore; it hasn't been a home since Nishi died. It's a cold house, a jail made of invisible skeleton ribs. Junichuro does a final cleanup of the house, putting everything where it belongs. He makes sure the cupboards are clean and the fridge is empty. He's always been a neat man, perhaps too neat. This no longer matters.

Once he is happy with how the house looks, he pads into his sitting room and leans the new business card against a book on the bookshelf. He approaches the beautiful samurai sword displayed on the wall. It's a family heirloom, worth millions of yen, but he has never been tempted to sell it. Gazing at its cold steel makes him think of warriors and bloodshed; love and heartbreak. It's a cruel world. He takes it down from the wall and polishes it with a soft cloth. Silence creeps inside his ears and muffles them; his eyes water, but Junichuro does not cry. The silence is getting more intense now, and he feels as if he is drowning in it. He places the carved handle of the sword on the floor and holds the razor-sharp tip in his palm, directing it slowly and thoughtfully to press into his torso. The blade bites into his skin, and he closes his eyes. Soon Junichuro will be with Nishi, and the world will be set right again. In his mind's eye,

Nishi's face smiles down at him and gives him the courage to press his weight against the blade, but just before he's about to fall on the sword, the business card slips off the shelf and flutters down to the floor. A white butterfly. The distraction makes him hesitate.

What am I doing? There's nothing good or honourable about this.

He lets go of the sword, and he collapses next to it, crumpling into a ball. He stays there, lying motionless in the dark, until his body is cold and full of aches.

The next day, Junichuro wakes up sore, stiff, and utterly desolate. He no longer has a job to go to. Not wanting to let his colleagues down, he had resigned in preparation for his suicide. There is no food in the house, just the suffocating silence of failure. He picks the white business card up off the floor and dials the number, scheduling an appointment for that afternoon. He leaves the house key beneath the pot plant outside the front door, just in case his daughter decides to return home. It's a years-old habit he has not yet broken.

Showered and dressed, he makes his way to a noodle bar for lunch and then to the offices of The Family Romance of Neurotics. It's a stylish building inside and out. Junichuro appreciates the clean lines of the architecture and the uncluttered interior. He is anxious, but the minimalism comforts him.

"Ohayō Misutā Matsumato," says the man who receives him. He's wearing neat but informal clothes which look too casual for the smart surroundings. Maybe Junichuro is just used to his own office, and the high-tech charnel house, where everyone wears expensive suits.

"I'm Yamamura. You can call me Yama for short. I'm glad you came in today."

They settle in a reception room, and Yamamura pours them both some fragrant tea.

"We can help you," he says. His fingers are slender and elegant.

"I miss my wife," says Junichuro. "I miss my daughter."

"We can help you with that," says the young man. "The manager at the charnel house sent through your wife's file. We have all the data we need."

"I'm not interested in robots," says Junichuro. "And I don't want those organic DNA clones, either."

"We don't manufacture stand-ins," says Yamamura. "We enlist them. The Family Romance of Neurotics is a relative replacement service. We use actors to play the part."

"Actors?"

"Very good actors. People with kind hearts. Would you like us to supply you with a new wife and daughter?"

"That sounds too good to be true," says Junichuro.

"Well, it'll only be for a few hours, of course. And they'll be pretending to love you; don't expect any authentic emotions to surface. And you're not allowed to touch them unless they initiate contact. Even then, it will be limited to hugs and hand-holding."

Junichuro thinks of the last years with Nishi. How many times had he hugged her, or held her hand?

"If you like them, we can reach an agreement regarding a regular visit."

Junichuro feels overwhelmed by the possibilities. "People do this? Your clients pay you to arrange fake relatives?"

"They're not fake, Misutā Matsumato. They're as human as you or I. Sometimes a client just needs a certain person in his or her life, and we're happy to provide that service. I recently facilitated a reunion between an engaged couple who had broken up because the bride's mother disapproved of the groom. We arranged for a stand-in mother of the bride and the wedding went off without a hitch."

Junichuro raises his eyebrows. "You were there?"

Yamamura smiles. "Yes. We go to a lot of weddings. They are our bread and butter. Sometimes, I even play the groom!"

"You're an actor, too?"

"That's how I started the business. A friend of mine—a single mother—wanted to get her toddler into a prestigious preschool, but both parents had to be present at the interview. I volunteered to go with them and play the part."

"Did the child get accepted?"

Yamamura laughs. "No, unfortunately not. He wouldn't even look me in the eye. But that was the day that sparked this," he gestures at the building. "It's good money but that's not why we do it. It's an extremely rewarding business to run."

"You were the groom at a stranger's wedding?"

"A client's wedding, yes," he says. "Sometimes I feel as if I am really getting married! Organising a Neurotic wedding is just as much hard work as a regular one, and by the time I kiss the bride at the ceremony we have usually bonded a lot."

"But why do they pretend to get married?"

"To get nagging parents off their backs? To get rid of a persistent ex-lover? Because they've always wanted a big wedding but have never met the right person? Each client has his or her own set of unique reasons. We're just here to help."

Junichuro walks all the way to his old office so that he can have time to think. When he finds his former boss, he asks if he can retract his resignation. A new face in a business suit is sitting in his office. There are toys on his desk. "Sorry," says his previous employer. "We've already hired a replacement."

"It's a strange world," says Junichuro, then leaves the air-conditioned office behind.

The daylight fades as Junichuro walks home. He's not used to the exercise, and his legs ache by the time he returns to his house. He is rooted to the spot when he sees the lights are on; there is friendly chatting going on inside. His house has been cold and quiet for so long. Junichuro walks cautiously to the front door, where someone had budged the pot plant in order to retrieve the key. He only notices now how the plant, a purple-flowered andromeda, is blooming. He wonders what else he has missed whilst being surrounded by the gloomy mental fog that has shrouded him since his wife's death.

When Junichuro opens the front door, he smells the distinct aroma of *okonomiyaki*, his favourite kind of savoury pancake; the type of pancake his wife used to make for him. He stands there, with the door open, unsure how to proceed into his own house, which is suddenly warm and welcoming.

"Churo?" comes a welcoming voice from the kitchen. "Is that you?"

Junichuro feels sweat break out under his arms. What has he done?

An attractive middle-aged woman with dark hair and sparkling eyes comes around the corner. She wipes her hands on a cloth and throws it over her shoulder.

"Churo!" she says again, "close that door and come out of the breeze."

She is around Nishi's age and weight and is wearing a simple, flattering dress with a small polka dot print that he's sure Nishi would have liked.

"Papa!" says a voice behind him, making him jump. He's on edge, and seeing strangers in his house adds to his feeling of discomfort. A jacket is draped unceremoniously on the back of a chair. There is a handbag on the side table. Junichuro turns to look at the young woman who had just called him. Like the woman cooking pancakes, she is a close match to his daughter: slender, with almond eyes. She hugs him, and he awkwardly returns the embrace. Her hair smells like apple blossoms.

"Papa," she says, "I've missed you! It's so wonderful to see you!" She pushes him playfully on the shoulder. "You're late! We expected you at sunset."

"Set the table, please," calls the woman in the kitchen. "The food is ready."

Junichuro washes his hands, and they sit down to dinner. His spine is straight and he finds it difficult to join in the banter. Everything feels surreal, and he wonders if he is dreaming.

"Oh," says the stand-in wife. "My name is Airi, but you can call me Nishi if you like."

"I'm Fumiko, but you can call me Chie," says the young woman.

Junichuro choked on a piece of mushroom, and without hesitating, Airi stood up to pound him on the back.

"Papa? Are you okay?" Fumiko passes him a glass of water. "Did I say something wrong?"

"No," Junichuro says, coughing. "I just—"

"It'll take some getting used to, having us around." Airi's hands rest on his shoulders, which relax slightly under her warm palms.

Fumiko puts her chopsticks down. "Would you like us to leave?"

"No," says Junichuro, taking a swig of water. "No. I'd like you to stay."

During the awkward tour of the house, Airi notices the Samurai sword displayed on the wall and gasps. "It's beautiful," she says, reaching for it.

Junichuro grabs her hand. "It's cursed," Junichuro replies. "You must never touch it."

The first date cost twenty thousand yen, and when Yamamura phoned Junichuro the next day to check on how he had enjoyed it, Junichuro requested a regular schedule where the women would visit three times a week. They agreed on a price and ended the call satisfied with the transaction. The next time the stand-in wife and daughter visited, it felt less awkward, and the conversation wasn't as stilted as before. Junichuro didn't choke on his food, and the women even laughed at a joke he told, which he wasn't used to, so it made him blush. On subsequent meetings, Junichuro gives them advice about saving money and investing. Sometimes he would buy them small gifts: tokens of his appreciation. A dress for Airi, a bracelet for Fumiko. Mostly, Airi cooks for them, but sometimes he would take them out to a restaurant. They become so comfortable with each other after a while that they don't even need to talk. They sit on the couch together, watching a movie or laughing at a game show. The women drop their pretences and feel free to act like themselves. One night they watch a movie about a father and daughter, and Junichuro finds himself switching off the television and putting his face in his hands. Still, he does not cry.

"What's wrong, Papa?" asks Fumiko.

"My daughter, Chie," says Junichuro. "We had a terrible argument. She moved out before Nishi died, and I haven't seen her since."

"All daughters need their fathers," says Fumiko. "You must phone her. She is waiting for your call."

"I don't know about that," he says.

"Fumiko is right," says Airi. "You must phone her."

Junichuro understands that because Fumiko is not his real daughter, he is less strict with her. They enjoy a closer relationship than he does with his flesh and blood. He is also more easygoing with the house when they are there. When Airi leaves her jacket lying around, or her hairbrush, Junichuro does not scold her as he would have, his wife. Junichuro's stand-in family makes him realise that he was too exacting with his family, too uptight. He understands with a feeling of sincere regret that he had been a cold husband and father. He hands the remote control to Fumiko.

"It's okay," she says, hugging him. "We'll watch something else."

· · ·

Junichuro is filled with a new purpose. He makes an appointment to see Yamamura at *The Family Romance of Neurotics*.

"Is there a problem, Misutā Matsumato?"

"Not at all," says Junichuro. "Not at all."

"The women tell me you are a wonderful man."

They drink tea while Junichuro tells Yamamura how happy he is with the service.

"I'd like to join the team," he says.

Yamamura sets his teacup down. "Join?"

"I'd like to help people the way Airi and Fumiko have helped me."

Yamamura claps his hands together. "Hai!" *Okay.* "When can you start?"

Junichuro's first job is to accompany an anxious pregnant woman to the doctor. The father of the baby has left her, and Erina needs support for the obstetrician appointments. He holds her damp hand as they look at the ultrasound screen together. They celebrate when the doctor says it is a healthy baby girl and get a printout each, to put on their fridge doors. He phones Erina now and then to ask how she is feeling, and check if she is taking her prenatal supplements. On another job, Junichuro stands in as a husband for a woman whose partner doesn't listen to her. He takes her out for *sake* and dumplings and listens carefully to what she has to say, and how she feels about the important and not-so-important things in life. He is empathetic and never gives advice; he is just there to listen and offer encouragement. This is another lesson for him, and he wishes he had learnt it before he pushed his wife and daughter away. Another job entails Junichuro to scold a high-ranking corporate director who is feeling demotivated in his career. He spends company money on hostess clubs and golf instead of doing his work, and he wants someone to reprimand him for it. Junichuro finds himself slamming his fist into the expensive boardroom table and yelling at the man, rebuking him for his lack of discipline. The director is satisfied with the treatment and adds a generous tip to the bill, with which Junichuro buys a teddy bear for Erina's baby and a ring for Airi. For the first time in years, he feels hopeful for the future, even happy.

The next job is significantly more difficult. The husband of a woman who has had an affair wants the lover to apologise to him. Junichuro is a loyal man; he knows it will be challenging to play this part. He prepares himself on the way to the appointment, trying to get into character as he had been taught in the training programme at The Family Romance of Neurotics. He would offer the man his sincere apologies; he would grovel if need be. Junichuro thinks of all the regrets he has in life and lets the emotions sit high in his chest, waiting to be spilt. When he arrives at the apartment, he is nervous. He paces the corridor and wipes the perspiration from his brow.

You can do this, Junichuro, he hears Nishi say. *You can do this.*

Junichuro knocks on the door and stands back, waiting for the angry husband to answer. The door flies open, and Junichuro immediately gets to his knees, apologising and begging for forgiveness. When he looks up, he sees the man is covered with bulging veins, prison ink and gangster tattoos, and his biceps are like rocks. Junichuro's blood runs cold. The man is a Yukuza, and he's furious. Everyone in Japan knows that if you make a member of the Yakuza angry, your life is as good as over.

Junichuro's gaze rests on the man's left hand and notices he's missing a small finger. Adrenaline washes through him like a bucket of cold water. The gangster reaches into his pocket. Expecting a knife, Junichuro jolts and moves to shield his face, but there is a flash of light before he does so. The gangster puts his phone away. He now has a picture of the man he thinks cheated with his wife.

Junichuro arrives home shaky and emotional. Airi is there to pour him a warm brandy and comfort him.

"Don't worry," she tells him, touching his shoulders the way she does. "Everything will be fine."

Junichuro brims with gratitude. He falls to his knees and brings out the ring.

"Marry me," he says. "Please."

Airi's hand flies to her chest. "What?"

"We are happy together, aren't we? Marry me."

"I wasn't expecting this." She takes a step back.

Realising his mistake, Junichuro springs up, fumbling with the ring with desperate fingers. He puts it back in his pocket.

"Ignore the ring," he says. "Ignore the foolish proposal. All I really want is you and Fumiko to stay here with me. I have enough room."

"I wasn't expecting this," repeats Airi, looking disappointed. Her look sends a sharp pain across his chest.

"I have learnt what is important in life now," says Junichuro. "Family is everything. But sometimes family isn't blood. I love you, Airi. Move in with me. Then it can be real."

"It is already real," says Airi.

"Not while I'm paying for your services," he says.

Airi smiles sadly and picks up her handbag. She walks towards the door. He has broken protocol, and now he probably won't see her again.

"Just think about it, Airi, please," says Junichuro. "The key will be under the pot plant, where it always is. Let yourself in, and make yourself at home. I'll make *okonomiyaki* for dinner."

When Junichuro wakes up, his eyes click open and the cold-water-dread is still sloshing inside him. He stares at the ceiling, thinking of Nishi, Airi, Yamamura, Fumiko, and Chie. He sits up and phones his daughter. She doesn't pick up, so he leaves a voice message.

"Chie, my beloved daughter. I am so sorry for the way I behaved. We should never have fought. You are a wonderful young woman and mature enough to make your own decisions. I know I have been difficult, but I understand now what is important. Please allow me to make it up to you. The andromeda is flowering, and the key is under the pot. You are always welcome here at home. I'm proud of you, and I love you."

He hopes she'll phone him back, or even come home for a visit. In the meantime, he has a job to do. He arrives at the maternity ward with the teddy bear and a bunch of yellow tulips. He finds the ward number of Erina, the pregnant woman he has been supporting, and wends his way through the antiseptic maze of white-tiled corridors. He hears her shouting from five doors down and picks up his pace. When he falls through the door, he sees Erina's flushed, perspiring face.

"Junichuro!" she says. "You made it!"

"I wouldn't miss it!" He fills a vase with water. "Are you in pain?"

"Pain is too subtle a concept for what I feel," she says, grinning, but then a contraction tears the smile off her face.

Junichuro shoves the tulips into a jug and rushes to Erina's side, not caring that it looks untidy on the hospital windowsill. "I'm here for you," he says, and she almost breaks his knuckles when the next contraction arrives. The hours in the ward pass excruciatingly slowly, but once they get into the delivery room everything speeds up, and people begin rushing around them, asking terse questions and instructing her when and how to push.

"You can do it, Erina," he says, remembering the birth of his own daughter, and how apprehensive Nishi had been. A part of him wants to rewind his life so that he could be a better husband and father, the other part—the stronger part—tells him he is exactly where he belongs.

When the baby arrives, choking and wailing, the doctor lifts the infant for Erina to see, and they are both overcome with emotion. Junichuro and Erina weep together, and when the baby is wrapped up and put on Erina's chest, they cry some more. The world is suddenly a painfully beautiful place, full of hope and despair and a strange, searing joy. Junichuro cries for his late wife, his prodigal daughter, and the future they'll never share. He cries for Airi and Fumiko, who had shown him what it was like to love again. The weeping allows Junichuro to break the bonds that had tethered him to his trauma, and his tears twist his heartache into a rising sense of purpose.

Junichuro leaves Erina to care for her new baby, kissing her forehead and promising to visit soon. As he heads home, he can't help feeling a bubbling sense of excitement in his stomach. Will Airi be there, cooking pancakes? Will Chie finally visit? He feels so different, now, and the world looks bright with possibility. He stops outside his house when he sees the kitchen and living room lights on, and it reminds him of the first night he met Airi and Fumiko. He had been awkward, but now he feels fluid and driven. The andromeda pot has been moved; the key is missing. The door is slightly ajar. He pushes it open the rest of the way and sniffs the air for the aroma of *okonomiyaki* or apple blossoms, but smells neither.

"Airi?" he calls.

The house is silent; that buzzing silence that climbs right into your ears and unsettles you. Junichuro then understands who is in his house. Instead of running, he takes off his shoes and walks through to the living room.

The Yakuza is there, his four-fingered hand wrapped around the jade handle of the cursed samurai sword. Without uttering a word, he knows the tattooed man is there to exact retribution for his wife's disloyalty. Junichuro is unarmed and full of grace. He knows he can fight, but he will not win. Instead, he drops to his knees before the street warrior and clasps his hands together, waiting for the finality of the cold, cursed steel. He thinks of the small buddha next to Nishi's high-tech glass grave in the charnel house in downtown Tokyo; thinks of the beautiful wash of autumnal colours as the LEDs change according to the seasons. There is a swishing sound. The last thing Junichuro sees is Nishi's shooting star, and he is happy.

~

10

SISTERS

The first time I became suspicious of my nanny was when I stalked her on Facebook. I don't know what made me look at her profile, but something about her photos made me feel uncomfortable. It became a bit of an obsession, always scrolling for new posts. In real life, Megan appeared wonderful, and Charlotte, my three-year-old, loved her.

I couldn't put my finger on why her social media posts unsettled me.

"Do you ever, you know, feel weird around Megan?" I asked my husband one morning as I pulled on my skinny jeans. They seemed tighter than usual.

Scott was adjusting his hair in the mirror. "Yes."

I froze. "Really?"

"Yes."

"What is it?" I asked, my stomach contracting.

"Well, it's really quiet when she's here, right? The kitchen is clean. And the house is tidy."

"Ah, shut it," I said, and tossed the closest thing at hand, which happened to be my pyjama pants. It landed on his head and only seemed to encourage him. He turned around and put on his fake ethereal voice.

"It's like ... a parallel universe," Scott said, making spirit fingers. "So peaceful."

"Feck off," I said. Unfortunately, there was nothing left to throw at him.

The hard truth was that life was a whole lot easier when Megan was around. Scott and I were both sleeping through the night for the first time in years. The toddler tantrums stopped, the laundry was done, and the kitchen didn't look like a small but effective explosive had been recently detonated in it. Why couldn't I just let go, and enjoy it? Was I really that uptight? Or was it envy? Sometimes I caught Scott glancing at Megan in an appreciative way. Megan was ten years younger than I was, and she had the body to prove it.

"She looks like you," Scott had said in a throwaway comment when we'd been searching online for a good match. "You could be sisters."

He had a point. We had the same long, dark, straight hair (hers was fuller and glossier), the same figure (hers was slimmer) and the same green eyes. Maybe I felt uncomfortable because we looked so similar. Perhaps it was the "uncanny valley" effect, where you get a weird emotional response from looking at an AI bot that appears too human. Now, I wasn't saying that Megan was a robot, but she may as well have been, with that tiny waist of hers, unfailing smile, and perfect skin. She was a decade younger, and unravaged by pregnancy, breastfeeding, and sleep deprivation.

No, I told myself. *I'm not envious at all.*

I Googled my nanny because she seemed too good to be true. Even her name sounded fake. Who names their daughter Megan Morris? There were no search results apart from a rather milquetoast Facebook profile, and all the details she had supplied in her CV matched up with what I saw there. Still, something about it made me feel uncomfortable. Was it my natural instinct, warning me that something was wrong? Or was I just tired, and envious of a woman who seemed to have unlimited energy (and perky tits)? Either way, I made sure to check in on her social media regularly, but this didn't stop the steady erosion of my life.

At first, it was the smallest of things that would go missing: my hairbrush; a framed photo; a pillow. Sometimes the absent objects would be Charlotte's. They would always be returned. I couldn't say for sure it was Megan borrowing the items, but there seemed to be no other explanation. Scott said I was mad, but I was used to that.

"What would Megan want with a photo of Charlotte?" he asked. He chuckled, but I could tell he didn't find it very funny. He had been acting strange recently—jumpy around the nanny—but, in his defence, so had I.

Maybe it was because of that evening I'd arrived home early to find them sharing a bottle of my favourite wine and laughing uproariously. Perhaps he felt guilty about that. Megan didn't seem worried at all. I was happy they got on, and I'm not one to begrudge anyone a great bottle of Shiraz, but I found it inappropriate. I may have overreacted, but I wasn't sorry; I didn't want Megan or Scott to think that it was okay to get drunk together while I was at work.

"We weren't doing anything wrong," said Scott, who seemed confused by my outburst.

"Good," I said. "Then you have nothing to feel guilty about."

There was a shortlist of things that unnerved me that had nothing to do with Scott. Charlotte crying for Megan in her sleep. Charlotte eating her vegetables when Megan cooked them. Charlotte wanting Megan to brush her teeth, brush her hair, lift her out the bath.

What is wrong with me? I wondered. But I knew the answer. There was nothing wrong with me—apart from feeling perennially overwhelmed—it was just that Megan was a nicer person.

One evening I asked Charlotte what she'd like to drink with dinner—reheated macaroni cheese—and she had replied "Gin and tonic."

I laughed out loud. "You're three," I told her. "Three-year-olds don't drink gin and tonic."

She looked put out by this. "Daddy lets me."

"You're so silly," I said, still smiling. "Daddy wouldn't. Also, he doesn't know where the gin is."

"Megan knows," my daughter said.

I stopped smiling.

"Megan makes us tonics at the picnic."

"What picnic?"

"Went to the park yesterday. Went on the slide."

I imagined Scott and Megan splayed out on our picnic blanket in the dappled shade, drinking out of a shared flask, laughing while they watched Charlotte play.

When Scott arrived home there was a bottle of gin and a six-pack of tonic water waiting on the kitchen counter for him.

"What's this?" he asked, scratching his head. I felt like punching him for being such a clueless oaf. Most of the time, I loved him, but sometimes I despised him. I guess that's marriage for you.

"Charlotte said you guys were drinking G&Ts yesterday, at the park."

"Oh," he said.

"Oh?"

He noticed my anger. "I'm not doing this again," he said. "You need to get your jealousy under control."

"I'm not the one going on romantic picnics with the bloody babysitter." I felt like sweeping the glass bottles off the counter so that they would shatter on the floor.

"It wasn't romantic," he said. "I took Charlotte to the park. Megan came with."

"She's toxic," I said to Scott.

He raised his eyebrows at me. "Megan's not the one who's toxic."

I leaned back against the counter and closed my eyes. Scott came towards me and pulled me into a hug. I resisted at first; then surrendered. I was so tired and on edge, and being hugged felt good. My anger dissipated, but it didn't disappear. Afterwards, I hid the gin away.

Each time I thought we should terminate Megan's contract, I'd see how much Charlotte loved her, and I knew I wouldn't be able to do it. Charlotte was happy, Scott was happy. I couldn't allow my envy or paranoia to derail that.

One evening, as I arrived home after a demanding day at work, I could smell Scott's cologne on Megan. It was just the slightest hint, but it was there. "Where's Scott?" I snapped.

Megan paused in the hallway, Charlotte clinging to her like a baby monkey. "I don't know," she said. "Showering?"

I looked at my watch. "At six p.m.?"

She shrugged and carried Charlotte to the kitchen for dinner. Something was going on, but I didn't know what.

Sometimes Megan would be over-familiar with me. She'd swing her arm around me, or touch my hair. Make me hot chocolate. Wear a cardigan or scarf without asking.

"I love you," she'd say to Charlotte. "I love you more than anything. I wish you were mine."

"Did you hear that?" I'd hiss at Scott.

"Stop picking up *stompies*," said Scott. *Stompies* are discarded cigarette butts—it's a South African saying that means stop eavesdropping on things that are none of your business.

Megan would compliment me in a passive aggressive way. She'd say barbed things like "You look great with makeup on!" and

"Your hair looks so beautiful when it's washed." "Have you lost weight?" she'd ask, and I hated her for it.

When I rolled my eyes, Scott would shrug. "What?" he'd ask. He was probably thinking *women are so complicated.* Or maybe he thought I was just being a thorny bitch.

One day, Megan gave me a photograph of the two of us, laughing together. The frame had the word "Sisters" printed on it. I don't know how she got the photo, or where it was taken. She hung it near the front door, and I hadn't had the heart to take it down, although every time I saw it, I felt a twinge of unease.

Things came to a head the next time I checked her Instagram profile.

"So THRILLED to say that I am PREGNANT," read the caption on a grainy picture of a 20-week ultrasound scan. This was slightly complicated by the fact that I was also five months pregnant. I was pale, nauseated, and swollen; Megan was her usual bubbly self. I resented her more than ever.

"When were you going to tell me?" I asked.

She had looked suitably contrite. "I was worried I'd lose my job."

What kind of a monster did she think I was? Although, to be fair, she was right. It would be the perfect time to get rid of her.

A few months later, Megan's Instagram photos showed her holding my daughter, wearing a jacket of mine. I felt as if she were trying to absorb me and take over my life.

It was time.

"You can't fire me," Megan said, holding her tiny belly. I had noticed with irritation that her waist hadn't grown an inch.

"Really?" I said. "Watch me."

I felt old and bitter in her presence. I just wanted her out. I didn't care if I was the toxic one; if I was bitter and twisted, she was the one who made me so.

I broke the news to her gently, and without pleasure. I didn't enjoy the fact that I was dismissing my daughter's favourite person, or that our house would return to its former post-apocalyptic state.

"You can't fire me," Megan said again.

"Yes, I can. I'll pay you for three months' notice."

"No," she said.

"Six months." It was my final offer.

"I don't want to leave you," Megan wheedled. "I love your family. I love Charlotte as if she were—"

"Don't say it."

"And *she* loves *me*," said Megan.

Anger climbed up my throat. I wanted to throttle her. I wanted to see her face turn purple. "Get out," I whispered.

She stood her ground; her eyes shone with malice. "I've got a rape kit on Scott."

"Shut up," I said. Reeling, furious, I had to shove my hands into my pockets to stop myself from slapping her.

"I know it's hard to hear," she said. "But it's true. It's at the police station. They've got the evidence in safekeeping if I ever want to press charges."

"He would never," I said.

Megan pouted. "You know he would."

It was her trump card, and I had to fold. I stared at her. We were twin images, hands resting on our bellies. "I knew it," I said to her. "I always knew there was something wrong with you."

When Scott got home, I launched into him, hitting him and pounding his chest. He grabbed my wrists and shouted at me to calm down. Charlotte began to cry. The house was already a minefield of LEGO bricks, half-eaten apples and hair clips.

"How could you?" I shouted at him. "How could you?"

My hair was a nest; mascara tinted my cheeks.

"I'm so sorry," Scott said, sitting down, dropping his face into his hands. "I'm so, so sorry."

"Megan says you raped her."

He looked up sharply. "What?"

"You raped her?" I was broken inside. "She has proof."

Scott shook his head. "No." He stood up again and took my chin firmly in his hand. "No, that never happened."

Charlotte was howling. Scott went to calm her down and put her to bed; then he fixed himself a whisky and a glass of milk for me. We sat in the living room, looking mournfully at each other. I couldn't touch the milk; I felt like splashing it in his face.

"The night you had that client dinner at Sasha's," he said, throwing the whisky back, and grimacing.

My jaw was tightly clamped as I kept the tears back. It was five months ago.

"I was asleep," Scott said. "I heard you shower and felt you climbing into bed."

I had not showered that night. I remember because I had been too exhausted after the presentation.

"You got into bed and rolled on top of me. You were wearing your silk pyjamas. And perfume."

"What?" I said. I felt like I was choking.

"I only really woke up when it was too late. I had already…"

I sat still, trying to breathe, trying not to hyperventilate.

"Stop," I said. "Just stop."

"It was too late," he said. "Even her hair smelt like yours."

"She's pregnant," I said. "*Five months* pregnant."

"As soon as I realised, I told her to leave."

"Why didn't you tell me?" I demanded.

"I felt guilty. She apologised. Said she must have misread my signals. I felt it was my fault."

"It wasn't," I said.

"I don't know." Regret washed over his face. He rubbed the stubble on his cheeks. "I think there were … signals."

I glared at my husband, hating every inch of him. "She's got a rape kit. She's going to press charges if we fire her."

"Then we can't fire her," he said.

If Scott went to jail, Charlotte would grow up without a father. I put my hand on my swollen stomach. The baby would grow up without a father. It was too much.

"What do we do?" he asked.

"We go to the police," I said.

Scott shook his head. "It's too risky."

"She's a psychopath. She is NOT staying in this house."

"Of course not," said Scott. "Of course not."

I threw the milk down the drain. "You created this problem," I said. "You fix it."

I scrubbed myself in the shower as if I had been the one who was violated. In a way, I had been. I felt sick thinking of how Scott and I had made love in the last five months. Everything I looked at seemed tainted by Megan, as if she had been a feral cat and sprayed everything in my territory. Even my pregnancy seemed tainted, and I detested her for that.

I washed every square inch of my skin and then rubbed it dry. I put on my most modest pyjamas but still felt somehow contaminated. I felt like smashing things; I felt like screaming. I hated Megan Morris more than I had ever hated anyone. I got into bed and waited under the covers, waited for my husband to come back and tell me that he had taken care of the problem.

I woke up to screaming. It was Charlotte. I ran to her bedroom and lifted her out of her cot, my heart racing, my ears buzzing. I swayed and shushed her, trying to calm her down. I felt disorientated. Where was Scott? Had Megan left?

"Meggie," Charlotte cried. "Meggie."

Of course, Megan had been the one to see to Charlotte if she woke up in the night. I remembered the time Charlotte had smacked my cheek because I wasn't Megan. The memory still stung.

"Did you have a bad dream, Charlie?" I asked.

She nodded, her cheeks wet with tears, and I hugged her closer, trying to comfort her with the warm substance of my body.

"No such thing as monsters," I said, quoting one of her favourite books. She closed her eyes and fell asleep in my arms. I was about to put her back in her cot but decided against it. Instead, I carried her to Megan's room to check that it was empty—it was —and then to the living room, where Scott was sleeping under an old blanket. I put Charlotte in our bed and kissed her soft, damp cheeks. I felt so close to her in that moment, and it made me feel better about everything else.

"It's going to be okay," I whispered. Two lies in two minutes. I snuggled deeply into her, my lips on the back of her sweet-skinned neck, and we slept.

Scott looked terrible the next morning, but I didn't feel sorry for him. I was glad he had dark circles under his eyes and mussed hair. I wondered if I'd ever forgive him for what he had done. I checked Megan's room again, and it had been completely emptied. I wondered how Scott had gotten rid of her, but was afraid to ask. The answer came later in the day when I was trying to pay off my credit cards. Charlotte had a meltdown, flinging herself on the kitchen floor. She wanted water. I gave it to her in a purple cup, which had in her eyes been a disaster of unmitigated proportions, as she had wanted it in a pink cup.

Giving up, I left her on the floor to scream and bang her heels. I wished I could do the same. When I finally was able to focus on my laptop screen, I noticed that R250,000 had been transferred from our access bond. So that's how Scott had gotten rid of her. It chilled me to the bone.

I checked Megan's social media and saw she had already started spending our money—she had some new baby clothes and a designer pram, and included the obligatory bump shot. "Sixteen weeks to go!"

Megan Morris—or whatever her name was—had utterly played us. She was nothing less than a predator, and I hated her with a white-hot fury. I thought of all the times she had held my daughter, sung to her, whispered in her ears. I felt sick, and I dashed to the sink and retched into it, but nothing came up. Charlotte fell quiet. I turned and saw that she had fallen asleep on the hard timber floor. My watch said it was two hours past her nap-time; no wonder she was behaving badly. I couldn't even remember my toddler's nap-time and I had another baby on the way. I didn't know how I would cope without a nanny. I sat down on the floor next to Charlotte and cried.

Later, I received a text from an unknown number: *I was never after your money.* I didn't reply.

Months passed, and my belly grew. Scott tried to atone for his infidelity by cooking dinner, cleaning the house, and spending extra time with Charlotte. Every time he did something nice for me, it was a reminder that he had been unfaithful. I knew I had to forgive him if I wanted the marriage to work, but I wasn't ready yet. I was still angry with him for letting "Megan Morris" happen to us. I raged at myself, too. I felt stupid and naïve for allowing her into our lives and not paying attention to my instinct, which had told me every day that there was something sinister about her. The house returned to its previous state of chaos, with toys strewn everywhere, an overflowing laundry hamper, and mouldy apple cores hiding in the crevices of the couch. As my due date approached, Charlotte regressed. She wanted to be on my lap all the time, climbing up my legs as I tried to meet my deadlines, demanding warm milk in baby bottles, and wetting her pants. Even though Scott was helpful, we hadn't reconnected since his confession. I felt alienated from him, and alone in my pregnancy.

"I know you're not going to want to hear this," Scott said.

I was eight months pregnant. My back was killing me, my bank account was empty, my anxiety was through the roof, and I wasn't sleeping. Scott was right. I didn't want to hear anything he had to say.

"We need to look for a new nanny," he said.

"Are you crazy?"

"I know, love. I know," he said gently. "But look around. Look at this place."

I didn't have to. I knew it was getting worse. Between the two of us, we just weren't keeping up with the relentlessness of full-time jobs, a home, and a toddler. Since Megan had left, we'd been in survival mode. Her room remained empty, despite my intentions to scrub it, hang new curtains, and assemble the new baby cot.

"You're about to pop," Scott said, gesturing at my ballooning abdomen.

"Thanks for that." He'd always had a way with words.

"I can only take a couple of days of paternity leave."

I glared at him. "That's convenient."

"It's not my choice, love. I'd rather be here with you."

"I'm not hiring another nanny," I said. He tried to argue, but I cut him off.

Judging from Instagram, Megan's bump was small and neat. My stomach muscles were pre-stretched from carrying Charlotte, and at nine months, people would—rudely—ask if I was expecting twins.

"Mama," said the car guard outside Pick n Pay. "You shouldn't be shopping."

Usually, unsolicited advice from random strangers made me bristle, but I took his point. I felt like a whale waiting to be harpooned, and not in a fun way. Leaning over to strap Charlotte into her carseat was practically impossible. *Okay*, I said to myself on the drive home—*no more grocery shopping*. I had already given up on picking toys up off the floor at home, even though I'd trip over the blasted things and swear in a way that would make a sailor blush.

"You said a bad word," Charlotte would say.

Get used to it, I thought, and gave her some juice in a pink cup. Later that day, the contractions began.

. . .

173

Scott arrived late at the birth clinic, but he was still in time to be sworn at and generally berated. He accepted it with good grace, and when I screamed in agony and effort for the last time before the baby arrived, Scott clutched my hand and wept.

"I'm sorry," he sobbed. "I'm sorry."

I hated that Megan had made her way into the intimate confines of the delivery room, and hated Scott for crying when I was the one in agony. But when I saw our beautiful new baby boy lifted, pink and squalling, I forgave Scott, and I told him so.

"Can we make it work?" he asked later, still holding my hand.

I was feeding the baby—Josh, we had named him. I looked up at my husband.

"Yes," I said, and I believed it. "I think we can make it work."

It felt like the start of a new life. Charlotte stopped her problematic behaviour, Josh was demanding but sweet, and Scott and I were tender with each other. He cleaned the entire house before our return, and his kindnesses no longer reminded me of Megan. I felt that I could eventually let her go. I even deleted the Instagram app from my phone, but not before having one last peek.

"Who is that?" asked Charlotte, making me jump. My fright jolted Josh, and he stopped feeding and started wailing.

"No one," I said, dropping my phone and trying to get Josh attached again.

Charlotte picked it up and looked at the screen. "Meggie!"

I gestured impatiently for her to hand the phone over, but she wanted to look at the selfie of Megan holding a bundle wrapped in a blue receiving blanket.

"Meggie has a baby?"

"Yes," I snapped, snatching my phone away. Of course, Megan was already back to her pre-pregnancy weight and grinning as if looking after a newborn was all sunshine and roses.

Charlotte's eyes welled up with tears, ready to throw a fit.

"Don't you dare," I said. I couldn't get the picture out of my head for the rest of the day.

When Josh turned a month old, Scott arrived home with a bouquet of roses and a gold-foiled bottle of bubbly. I froze and searched my brain. Was it my birthday? Mothers' Day?

"Oh," I said, guilt rising. "Happy anniversary."

He kissed me and told me we had lunch reservations at the new underground Japanese restaurant I'd been wanting to try. He'd organised a babysitter for the kids—his boss's daughter. Before I could argue, he stormed me with his thoughts.

"Lesley's great with kids. She babysits for loads of people at the office. If this works well, we can go out more often. It'll be good for both of us. You always say you feel we never do anything anymore."

It was true; I was craving a night out. I had been attached to Josh 24/7 for over a month, and I was ready to have a couple of hours out with Scott and a bottle of Cap Classique.

"I just feel nervous about—"

"I know," he said, leaning in for a hug. "But we won't be able to avoid nannies and babysitters forever."

The boss's daughter brought over books and a slab of chocolate. Lesley Johnson was slightly overweight and had frizzy hair. I liked her immediately. Within minutes Charlotte was introducing her to every stuffed animal she owned, and Josh slept in her arms.

"Ready?" asked Scott.

We had a wonderful lunch and a little too much bubbly before we realised our phones had no signal in the underground restaurant.

"Get the bill," I said. "I'll go outside so long to check my messages."

I stood in the sunshine and lifted my phone, checking the signal. No messages. I had escaped the relentless demands of my life for ninety golden minutes, and it felt good. Scott came out into the warm afternoon light, smiling.

He kissed me, and I felt connected to him again. His phone started ringing. Scott looked at it and frowned. "It's my boss."

I was instantly sober.

My phone beeped with three missed calls from Lesley. I looked up and saw the fear on Scott's face. He held the phone in one hand and pulled his hair with the other.

"What?" I shouted. I tried to book an Uber, but my hands were shaking too much. "What?"

"Johnson wanted to check if everything was all right."

"Why?"

"He said Lesley just called to ask if you had a sister. He told her you do."

My whole body went cold. I couldn't focus on anything. We had to get home.

Scott booked the Uber, and I dialled Lesley, but she wasn't picking up. When we pulled up, I was in such a hurry to get out of the car that I tripped and cracked my knees on the tarmac, grazing the skin. Reality seemed distorted: the trees in our front garden were electric green, and the sky felt like it was falling in. I couldn't get enough oxygen into my lungs despite my hyper-ventilating. We finally reached the front door and yelled for Lesley, who was shocked to see us in such a state. Hair standing on end, knees leaking blood.

"Where are the children?" I shouted. I didn't wait for her to answer. I ran into the house and checked Josh's cot. It was empty. "Josh?" I screamed, as if he would reply. "Charlotte?"

Scott was on the phone, panic-stricken. "It's an emergency!"

"Where is Josh?" I asked an ash-faced Lesley. "Charlotte?"

"Your sister took them for a walk," she said.

"My sister?"

Lesley pointed at the photo of Megan and me on the wall. *Sisters.*

Things began tumbling into place. The neat bump, the immediately flat stomach. The bundle of blankets in the picture with no trace of a baby's face, arms, or legs. Megan's pregnancy had been a lie, but she had told the truth about one thing: she hadn't been after our money, after all.

177

11

RED SCRIBBLE

Weeds fought their way through the cracked concrete slab only to wither and die. It was that kind of apartment building.

Dilapidated, abandoned, but not empty. Clues from former residents and passers-through remained, together forming a messy shrine to honour lives gutted or smashed off-course by the things that had taken place within the vandalised walls. Memento Mori.

K wasn't spooked; haunted buildings didn't frighten him. He had learnt early on that humans were infinitely scarier than the spirit world. It was one of the reasons he didn't charge for his side-hustle of paranormal investigation, despite living on the breadline. He didn't like it when people were frightened, especially children. He hated the idea of kids being scared.

K made his way through the small block of flats, sweeping his torch before him to avoid tripping over debris and garbage. Years ago, a fire had disembowelled half of the building, destroying the pipes and wires and other arteries that kept it alive. No one lived in Anvil House after that, and the remaining furniture had been looted or smashed up to be used as firewood. Squatters and drug addicts came and went, but no one ever stayed. A pervasive sense of malevolence cooled the air around K, and his breath turned to whirling grey mist.

K didn't make use of paranormal activity sensors or any other ghost-busting paraphernalia. He didn't need it. The doctors said his brain was damaged, and while he believed them—he had seen the x-rays, the scans, the MRIs with their cold blue lakes of defective grey matter—he didn't conceive of the head trauma injuries as a handicap, but as a superpower. Of course, he never told the neurologists that; he didn't want to get locked up in some bleak asylum. He had his methods of keeping his demons under control, but if he were to end up alone, in a straightjacket, he didn't fancy his chances much. Chasing ghosts was one way to stay sane in an insane world. That was another reason he didn't charge for his work. It benefited him as much as it did the person who sought him out. In most cases, he reckoned he needed the job more than the person trembling on the other side of the phone.

There was a sound, and K stopped in his tracks, listening. He guessed it was a lead pipe being struck in the distance. He shone his flashlight around, saw nothing unusual, and continued his slow investigation. The air got colder as he made his way towards the centre of the building. A feeling was drawing him further and further in; an emotional magnetic force. An invisible rope looped around his waist and squeezed his stomach as he made his way down the cliff face. The floor might have appeared horizontal, but K knew better. When he reached the epicentre of the cold energy, he stood in what used to be a family room. How did he know that, when there was no furniture? Nothing at all except some cracked syringes in the corner, and a bloodstained mattress at his feet that made his skin crawl. K took a deep breath, and then another. The rope felt too tight, and it made his stomach ache. What was it with this room? His mouth turned dry, and he became dizzy. He leaned against a dusty wall for support, and then he saw it. A built-in cupboard on the wall opposite, with large, irregular holes in place of the two handles, like empty eyes. The space beneath the eyes formed a gaping mouth. To some children, it might have looked like a monster, but to K, it was an old friend. A flashing light cut into his head, a razor memory: his father smashing his head with something dark and heavy. He had been knocked out, cheek-on-carpet, jaw unhinged. The cupboard face had kept him company. He was there when K lost consciousness and again when he woke up, as if keeping vigil.

K felt blinded as the brutal memory bit into him. Back pressed up against the wall, he slid down, and the floor came up to meet him. This was the room. He used to live here. Of course, there was a blur of other homes, too; dozens of them. K's father was forever moving the family around to dodge criminal charges and social workers. It's why no-one took K away when he was hospitalised over and over again for blunt-force trauma. Different cities, different hospitals, different people asking the same questions.

He's a clumsy boy, his mother used to say, breathing out a seemingly constant stream of tobacco smoke. *He's forever falling out of trees.*

K blinks away the claustrophobic images and focuses once more on his breathing.

Broken teeth, surgical screws in his jawbone and femur. A cheek so scarred, the other children called him Frankenstein.

He had two older sisters, but they disappeared. Eventually, K ran away, too.

He sat there, trembling, waiting for the ghost to appear. *Hoping* the ghost would appear.

Young, beautiful, long black hair, the caretaker of the neighbouring building had said. *But she's angry.*

"Why are you angry?" he asked the cold air that had now seeped into his bones. The ghost didn't answer. K lay down on the concrete and slept.

He dreamt of the ocean, which he had never visited before. Dreamt that there were words written in the sand. Instead of washing the words away, the rising tide added more and more. K couldn't make out what they said. When he woke up, he smelled gunpowder and blood. He began to search the thin walls. The bulb of his flashlight flickered. On the wallpaper of the flat next door, a name was written in red felt-tipped pen. It was at the height of a child and scrawled in loopy, immature handwriting.

Julie Manchester.

K snapped a quick photo, then read the name out loud. It had a ring to it, a tinny taste of familiarity. Did he know her? His childhood was mostly a blank. The doctors called it traumatic amnesia dissociation. His brain, battered into a survival state, buried his most painful memories. Sometimes one would try to surface, but K felt his psyche choke it before it bloomed, before it had the opportunity for its roots to cut any deeper.

K grasped the image of the red scribble like a lucky charm all the way home.

Julie Manchester.

It was easy to find her, triangulating various social media sites. He zoomed in to a photo he found and immediately felt guilty for invading her privacy. It was a public profile picture, but he couldn't help sensing he was intruding. He was, after all, studying the face of someone who had no idea he was doing so. He glanced at his watch, a cheap gadget he'd bought off a street vendor. Wristwatches had the habit of stalling the moment any kind of phantom appeared, never to recover. His latest cheapo was still ticking away—it was almost ten p.m.—confirming his suspicion that, despite the scent of gunpowder and blood, the ghost had not made an appearance at Anvil House while he was there.

Despite all odds, Julie Manchester agreed to meet him the next night. It was easy enough to comply with her demands: a crowded place with closed-circuit cameras and tight security. The Paradiso Casino was perfect. She sent him a text before she arrived, and when he felt his phone buzz in his jacket pocket, he thought she had decided against the meeting. Instead, it was a message saying her best friend would call the police if Julie didn't answer her phone in half an hour.

K set off the metal detector walking in; he always did. The bolts in his jaw weren't going anywhere. Sighing, they patted him down and let him in, and he ordered an iced tea at the cheap and cheerful bar. He probed his broken teeth with his tongue while he waited. You never get used to broken teeth.

When he felt Julie Manchester's gaze, the hairs on the back of his neck stood up. He turned in his chair and looked at her.

"You look just like him," Julie said. She looked unnerved. Too fragile.

"Like who?"

"Like your father."

K grimaced; it felt like a vicious punch in the stomach. The air left his lungs. "You're pale," he said. "Can I get you something to drink?"

She picked at her coal-coloured sleeves. "I'm not staying."

"Okay. I understand."

They stared at each other.

"Don't you remember me?" she asked.

"I remember your eyes." Violet irises that peeked out from under a dark fringe. He saw a picture in his mind of a frightened child, hiding under a table.

Julie crossed her arms tightly, as if she was cold, and threw her long hair back with a shake of her head. She took a step forward. "There were others, you know?"

The ache from the sucker-punch spread to K's lungs and heart. His mouth was dry again. "Other what?"

Julie kept quiet for a long minute. "Isn't that why you asked to meet me?"

"I'm sorry," K said. "I don't remember much about ... growing up."

Julie glared at him, then her expression softened. "That makes sense, I guess." The walls at Anvil House were thin.

The bartender gave K a suspicious look, but he didn't care.

"Who were the others?" He didn't want to know the answer, but it was his father who had brought them together, and he had to bear witness, no matter how painful it was.

"Anyone," Julie said. "Any young girl who he could convince to go into your flat. Into his bedroom."

K tried to swallow the burning blockage in his throat, but it wouldn't go down. "How many?"

Julie shrugged. "All I know is that I wasn't the only one. He used to tell me about the others."

K's lips turned down at the corners; his body flooded with toxic guilt, like poisoned oil in his veins. Nothing he could say would ever make any of it better. He apologised, anyway.

Julie sighed and let her thin arms fall to her sides as if surrendering. "Wasn't your fault. I told my parents, and they didn't believe me. How were *you* supposed to know?"

"I'm not like him," said K.

"I know," said Julie.

"Were we friends?"

Julie smiled for the first time. "You were my only friend. We used to climb onto the roof together. We'd eat Eskimo Pies."

"Eskimo Pies?"

"The other kids in the building had bikes, so we'd be left behind. We'd walk to the café on the corner and buy Chappies and Eskimo Pies."

The knowledge filled a long-empty part of K. He imagined the cold vanilla popsicle on his tongue, the warm, rough roof-tiles against his back, and the animal shapes in the shifting clouds. His childhood wasn't a vacuum, after all. Julie had imparted terrible knowledge, but also a gift.

"We should—" K said. "What I mean is, would you agree to press charges against him? Against my father?"

Julie's mouth fell open. "God. You really have no idea."

She was right. He didn't even know his real last name, never mind his father's. "I know a lot of things," he said. "I just don't know about my family."

"Your father's dead," Julie said.

"Oh."

For the first time in hours, he felt his shoulders relax. His stomach stopped hurting.

"He was killed by a woman," Julie raised her eyebrows. "No prizes for guessing why."

The pieces began to fall into place. The ghost had been drawn to the nucleus of K's father's evil—Anvil House—and in so doing, she had drawn K there, too. The red scribble.

"The woman," he said. "Did she—"

"She tracked him down. Shot him a few times and saved a bullet for herself."

K felt the invisible rope around his torso loosen; he unclenched his aching jaw. He glanced down at his watch. "It's been half an hour," he said. "Your best friend is going to call the cops."

Julie smiled. "There's no best friend. I just wanted you to think I'd be missed if you did anything to me. You could have been anyone."

K sensed her vulnerability, her hunger. He would be her friend.

"I won't do anything to you," he said.

186

The bartender is still watching him with an odd expression on his face.

"Would you like to get out of here?" K asked. "We can go for a walk."

"Okay," Julie said, threading a strand of long black hair behind her left ear. "I'd like that."

He stood up and offered her his hand. It was deathly cold, as he'd expected. K's watch had stopped half an hour ago, as soon as Julie Manchester had walked through the door.

12

IN THE HANDS OF GOD

We knew the new sister-wife would be trouble. Angus fell for her like a hammer at a circus tent, and we all felt in our hearts that something had shifted, and there'd be no going back. Ruth-Anne was blond and a little too beautiful, and after we met her for the first time, I saw the stars in my husband's eyes. He hardly ate any of Clara's lamb stew, even though she's the best cook in the family by far, and it had always been his favourite.

"Is this what he was like when he met me?" I asked Clara that night. Clara was the first wife—the legal wife—and matriarch. Angus thought he was the one who held the family together, but really, it was Clara. She was firm, loving, and steadfast. Sometimes my marriage to her felt more real, and more intimate, than my marriage to Angus. We had a bond that sister-wives in other plural families envied.

"Of course he was," Clara said. "It was love at first sight with you, Hannah. You know that."

I'm not sure I would have accepted Angus's marriage proposal if it weren't for Clara. She's the one who wooed me during the courting phase. After Angus had expressed his desire for me to join the family, the three of us got to know each other. After two seasons, I accepted.

"How will it work?" I asked.

"We'll decide on that together," said Clara.

Our plural marriage was successful because it was a true collaboration; we had a common goal, and all worked hard towards it. When I was having a stressful day with the children, I would wonder how non-plural families managed. Only one mother in a house seems a hard way to live. My parents were of the same faith, and they said it all the time: *It takes a village to raise a family.* Now I know why. Some days are just crammed too full of life, and you'd feel overwhelmed if you didn't have a sister to lean on. I thanked God for Clara every day. I'm not saying there was never jealousy, that would be dishonest, but Clara was always generous with Angus and me. Especially in the beginning, when I was getting used to the dynamics in the house. I was supposed to sleep in Angus's bed every second week, and I battled with that. Clara accommodated my insecurity by granting permission for me to spend any night of the month with him, even if she was the first wife, and it was her turn.

"Won't you miss him?" I asked. I didn't want to make trouble.

Clara laughed. "Angus and I have a solid relationship. He's not going anywhere. Besides, I'd appreciate the time to myself. I'm behind on my reading."

After a few weeks of borrowing Angus during Clara's turn, I realised I was no longer envious of their time together, and we went back to alternating beds every week. I picked a bunch of wildflowers for her, to say thank you, and she hugged me. I also came to realise how much I enjoyed my own company. On the nights I wasn't with Angus I felt liberated, and I appreciated the rare time on my own when I wasn't busy with the seven children in the house and the never-ending housework. I thought that I had conquered the problematic emotion of jealousy, but when Ruth-Anne arrived in our lives, I realised I had not.

We began the courting process, and I dreaded every encounter with Ruth-Anne. I found her superficial. She laughed too much, too loudly. And, yes, she was too beautiful. I pressed Clara for her opinion, but she was, as always, too gracious to concede that Ruth-Anne was anything but lovely. Eventually, at the risk of appearing unkind, I had to address it with Angus. I waited until he was in a good mood and then cautiously brought the conversation around to the impending engagement.

"I don't think Ruth-Anne is a suitable match for our family," I said. He looked alarmed. "I'm sorry," I blurted. "I wish it was different. I know you really like her."

"Like her?" he said. "I'm in love with her. And she's agreed to marry us."

His words cut through me like a ploughshare. I wanted to lie in bed and weep; instead, I stood there in our bedroom and stared at the carpet. I felt betrayed in the worst way. As a sister-wife, the only power you have is deciding who to accept into your family, and Angus was undermining that power.

"I was going to tell you and Clara tomorrow in our family meeting. I know it's difficult for you," Angus said. *You've always been the jealous one,* I imagined him thinking. *You're not emotionally mature enough to deal with another wife. This will be the lesson you need to overcome your inadequacies.*

"Our family is perfect," I said. "Are Clara and I not enough for you?" I loathed myself for saying it; loathed how panicky and vulnerable I felt. I wished I could have as generous a heart as Clara.

Angus looked unhappy. It wasn't the first time I had disappointed him, and my cheeks burned with shame.

"Please remember who we are, and why we do this," he said. "We are following the word of God."

I respected Angus deeply, but I disliked it when he brought the Lord into our arguments. If God was on his side, who could argue?

"God didn't choose Ruth-Anne," I said. I felt the scorpion sting of my spite.

"Of course He did," said Angus. "This is the Almighty's plan. Why else would she be in our lives?"

My skin continued to burn, and my throat swelled with all the angry words I could not utter. I grabbed my pillow and stalked out. *He can sleep alone tonight,* I thought. *Just him and his Almighty.*

Clara was peeling carrots when I joined her in the kitchen. I washed my hands and got to work. There was a lot of chopping to do in a household of ten people. I thought, not for the first time, that soon we'd have to invest in some industrial-size food appliances. As it was, cutting onions would leave us half-blind with tears. My five-year-old said it made his eyes melt, which had given Clara and me a good chuckle. She rolled out the pie pastry dough on the counter and sprinkled it with flour. I don't know where she learnt to cook, but she was a natural. I had once told her that being a housewife was a waste of her talents. She had laughed and said real work happened at home, that no other job would have as much meaning or impact as being a wife and mother. I envied how she never seemed to long for more. I swept the vegetable peels into the compost bin and wiped down the counters. It's not that I didn't like cleaning; it was just that I felt I cleaned the same things a hundred times a day. I secretly looked forward to the time the children would fly the coop and the clean things would stay clean.

"Keep those bones," Clara said, and I frowned at her, raw chicken bones in my hands. "Throw them into that pot on the stove. It'll make a good broth."

Clara's chicken broth was famous in our four-hundred-strong gated community. Cooked with organic garden produce and seasoned with love, it was said to cure everything from head colds to depression.

"I wish I could cook like you," I said.

"You have your talents," Clara said. She winked at me and slammed the oven door shut.

"Do I? It doesn't seem that way."

Sometimes I felt like a cheap knockoff of Clara, a flawed copy.

"Angus proposed to Ruth-Anne," I said. "She said yes."

Clara froze for a moment, then took off her apron and folded it neatly away. "Yes. He told me."

"Clara," I said. "You know it's not a suitable match."

"I know that Angus loves her," she said.

"It's not up to Angus!" I said, then looked around and lowered my voice. "It's supposed to be a family decision."

193

"Angus is the head of the family," she said. We stared at each other, and the broth boiled over on the stove.

While Angus and Ruth-Anne said their vows, with Clara and I as matrons of honour and witnesses, I gazed at my husband, remembering our own wedding day. It had been a similar set-up: a small gathering in the local church, a simple white dress that my mother had sewn, and a gold ring on my finger. I loved him and Clara so much, I was sure I'd be happy. Standing there at the altar for the second time, I felt that happiness slipping away, and I was powerless to stop it.

I'd always been taught to forgive, to look for the good, to keep peace in the home, so when Angus insisted on marrying Ruth-Anne, I forced all my feelings down until they formed a permanent heaviness in my stomach. Had my sense of freedom been an illusion? I knew people not of our faith found it difficult to understand polygamy. Some even thought of us as brainwashed, being kept under control by our manipulative husbands, but this was not the case in our family. We were bound by true, selfless love. Even if something happened to Angus, I was sure Clara and I would stay together.

"We have to make it work," said Clara, as we wilted at the modest wedding reception. We'd been cooking for hours the day before to have everything ready, and Clara had even made a cake.

I sighed into my empty cup. I'd had a sleepless night and the children's excited play outside grated my ears. "It's hopeless."

"Nothing is hopeless in the eyes of God."

I bit my tongue for what felt like the thousandth time. When

Ruth-Anne spoke to me, I smiled and replied in a gracious way, and Angus looked on approvingly. I prayed for patience and grace, and I begged God to open my heart.

Ruth-Anne moved in, and so did her ego. In her mind, being the third wife was a superior position. She was new; she was shiny goods. She'd clog up the shower drain with her long blond hair and expect me to clean it. She delighted in scolding Smarticus, our beloved tabby cat. Ruth-Anne wasn't interested in the children and refused to do any kind of childcare, citing her inexperience as a possible danger. If there was an extra cupcake, she'd eat it.

We hadn't gained a sister-wife, I thought. We'd gained another child, and an ungrateful one, at that.

Angus was so blinded by her shininess that he didn't see the extra work Clara and I were doing. Every time I ironed Ruth-Anne's clothes, I had the urge to scorch them, especially her favourite top which, though modest, was extremely flattering. There were other practical considerations, too: we could no longer all fit around the massive dining room table. The top-loader decided it was being overworked and gave up the ghost. Clara's favourite cast-iron casserole pot was no longer large enough. When we bought another one, they couldn't both fit in the oven at the same time.

"We need a new oven," I told Angus.

He looked surprised, perhaps at my business-like tone.

"We don't have money for a new oven," he said.

You should have thought of that before you decided to marry another wife, I thought. *You should have thought of the implications.*

"Make a plan," I replied. I knew I was being cheeky, but I didn't care. My resentment had hardened me, despite my prayers.

The next week, Clara was thrilled when Angus came home with a new oven that was twice the size of the old one. Later I found out the money had come from our allowances and I bit down hard on my rancour. Clara and I had been scrimping for months to afford a weekend away together, which was our annual tradition, but now the account was empty. When I confronted Angus about it, he shrugged. "I made a plan."

I prayed very hard that night.

While Angus and Ruth-Anne's relationship bloomed, ours faltered. When I was in bed with my husband, I imagined he wished I was Ruth-Anne. I felt self-conscious about my body for the first time in years, pulling the comforter up to cover my stretched skin and sagging breasts. I no longer wanted to plea-sure him because my heart was full of bitterness. It became a vicious circle and, after a while, we stopped making love. Some-times I wished that it wasn't my turn with Angus, even though my bed was already empty two weeks out of three. Sometimes I wished he and Ruth-Anne would move out and live somewhere else, and leave us in peace. My resentment towards Ruth-Anne did not go unnoticed. Clara implored me to leave it in the hands of God, and Angus called a family meeting so we could discuss my behaviour.

"My behaviour?" I asked. "What about Ruth-Anne's behaviour? What about the way she never helps around the house, never speaks to the children, never does a load of washing?"

"Ruth-Anne is still settling in," said Angus. "It's the honeymoon period. It was the same with you."

I looked at Clara, who nodded. "It's the same with every new wife," she said gently. "I made concessions for you. I cooked for you. I gave you unlimited access to Angus."

I remembered. It was true.

"Give it time," said Clara. "You'll see, we'll all be settled in soon enough."

But for once, Clara was wrong. Anyone who expected Ruth-Anne to start chipping in was sorely disappointed. She'd leave dirty mugs all over the house, plates with crumbs, candy wrappers. She began to put on weight because she'd lie and watch TV all day while we worked to keep the machine of the household running. There was always more to do, but Ruth-Anne was on a permanent holiday. Once I vacuumed under her feet and accidentally rammed her just-painted toenail. I was getting so clumsy! I dropped her pancakes on the floor one morning—no-one was watching so I just loaded them back on the plate—and I did eventually scorch that flattering top of hers. No matter how hard I prayed, the clumsiness remained.

When Ruth-Anne complained to Angus, he replied that it was time she began to wash and iron her own clothes, and running a vacuum around the house now and then would not go amiss.

"Bless her heart," Clara and I used to say to each other when we were annoyed with Ruth-Anne.

Ruth-Anne's behaviour deteriorated. Her moods would swing wildly from manic to depressed, and she'd stay glued to the couch for a week. On one of these days, we ran a deep, salted bath for her, and let her soak. Clara washed Ruth-Anne's hair, which she had impulsively cut short with the kitchen scissors a few days before. Her unpredictability unnerved me.

"She needs medication," I said to Angus.

"Leave it in the hands of God," he replied. He had been distracted lately. Work had been demanding, his second wife was no longer appreciative of his advances, and his third wife was proving difficult to manage. I scolded myself for the pleasure I felt in Ruth-Anne's pain. *Schadenfreude*, they call it. I knew it wasn't virtuous, but I couldn't help that little stab of spiteful enjoyment I got from seeing the shininess erode to rust.

On a day she couldn't keep still, Ruth-Anne left her couch and came to watch the children playing outside. Angus had built them a beautiful treehouse which they spent hours scaling the tree to reach, then squealed down the slide, or climbed down the knotted rope that hung from the timber beams. It was a cheerful scene until I saw Clara's three-year-old daughter, a daring girl who enjoyed rough-and-tumble with her brothers, wrestling with my son at the entrance of the treehouse. They were arguing about whose turn it was to slide down.

"Stop!" I called as a raced over. "Mary! Jonathan! Stop!"

I didn't get there in time. My son, who at five was twice the size of Mary, pushed her aside, not realising she'd tumble off the side. She hit the ground with a thump and an eye-watering crack. Then there was silence. I gasped, glancing up at my son. Realising what he had done, his hands flew up to his mouth and his eyes filled with horror. As I reached Mary, she began to wail, and I thanked God that she was still alive. The silence had been terrifying. Jonathan rushed down the slide to join me as I picked the screaming child up.

"Call Clara!" I told him. "Tell her to bring the keys for the truck.

We need to get Mary to the hospital."

Jonathan, white as new snow, turned to run inside, but Ruth-Anne caught him by the ear.

"You evil child," she said. "Look at what you've done."

Mary was screeching, so I wasn't sure I'd heard correctly. "Ruth-Anne," I said. "Let him go."

With her left hand, she let go of his ear, and with her right, she slapped my son so hard that he fell. The sound of the blow was louder than that of Mary's arm breaking, seconds earlier.

I wanted to scream. God help me; I wanted to hit Ruth-Anne back and see her lying on the ground. Instead, I stood rooted to the spot, pinned down by the trauma of the moment as my son sobbed into the grass. Clara ran out of the house, and when Mary saw her, she cried louder and started kicking.

"Hannah!" she cried, out of breath. "What has happened? You're as pale as death!"

I hung on to the struggling toddler. "We need to get to the hospital," I said.

In the family meeting, we discussed what had happened that day. Mary was sleeping in Clara's arms, a clean white cast over her broken arm. Jonathan sat next to me, his swollen face contrite. Angus looked disappointed in all of us, although I couldn't say why.

"It was an unfortunate incident," he said, putting down his mug of coffee.

My angry words bubbled up; I couldn't help it. Even prayer

would not keep them down.

"Ruth-Anne needs to know that she can't hit the children," I said. It was the mildest way I could put it, and every word took effort.

"As a member of this family, Ruth-Anne is allowed to discipline the children," said Angus. "In fact, it is expected of her."

"Discipline?" I demanded. "That wasn't discipline. That was abuse. Look at him! Look at my son's face!"

Jonathan was about to start crying again, so I pulled him up onto my lap and hugged his little body to mine and kissed his hair. If my hand were cool, I would have put it on his swollen cheek, but my whole body was hot and bothered by the emotion eddying inside me.

Angus sighed. It was his way of asking us to calm down. I felt the opposite of calm. I wanted Ruth-Anne out of our house and out of my life.

"Your son broke Mary's arm," said Ruth-Anne. "He has to learn there are consequences."

"They were playing!" I shouted. "It was an accident!"

I looked at Clara, thinking she would want me to settle my emotions, but she was staring blankly at the table, still shocked by her daughter's injury. It had been a difficult afternoon at the hospital. People not of our faith often treat us like aliens, or foreigners who don't understand English or science.

We're going to have to X-ray her arm, the nurse had said. *Do you know what that is?*

I've got a painkiller here for your daughter. Do you consent to this medicine?

I hesitated on that one. People of our faith weren't allowed pain medication. We were supposed to embrace pain and the lessons contained therein. Unless the condition was life-threatening, we weren't allowed medicine at all. Clara and I had discussed it on the way to the hospital. A plaster cast wasn't really *medicine*, we agreed. It was a tool, a prop. It was temporary. It wasn't strictly medicine, but we'd keep it hidden from the other townsfolk just in case. We'd make sure Mary wore long sleeves to church.

"A painkiller, Ma'am?" repeated the nurse.

"Is Mary in pain?" I asked.

The nurse sighed and placed a liver-spotted hand on her generous hip. "I wouldn't be asking permission for pain medication if she weren't in pain."

I looked around sharply, searching for Clara, who had gone to the bathroom.

"Yes," I said softly, nodding at the nurse. "Please give it to her."

I hoped she'd forget to write it on the chart.

I didn't know if Clara blamed me. I had been the one looking after the children, and it was my son who pushed Mary. She avoided eye contact at the family meeting that night.

"Clara?" I said. I needed to know that our relationship was okay. She looked up at me and blinked as if waking up from a daydream. Smarticus wound his tail around my legs and meowed. Angus sighed again and pinched the bridge of his nose as if a headache was approaching. The fact that the head of the house was not saying anything intensified my anger, and I felt like I might explode. Instead, I stood up, still clutching my son, and looked Ruth-Anne directly in the eyes. "Ruth-Anne. If you ever touch a hair on any of our children's heads again, I will make sure you are sorry for it."

Clara kept staring at the table. Ruth-Anne pursed her lips and glared back, so I left the room, taking Jonathan with me.

My son's bruise faded, but he refused to look at or speak to Ruth-Anne, and he wouldn't let me leave the house if she was there. I had to take him grocery shopping, which was already a momentous task. The cashiers always eyed us suspiciously as we loaded dozens of loaves of bread and packets of fruit onto the counter.

"You're throwing a party?" she asked.

"Nope," I said.

They always had something to say.

You're too skinny to eat all a-that.

You sure like bread, huh? An' you got enough cheese right here to start a cheese fac-tory!

You opening a res-tau-rant?

I had left my white hair cap in the car, hoping to blend in more with the other shoppers, but my waist-long hair and homemade dress still gave my faith away. It didn't help that Jonathan stared back at the people who looked at us.

"Why do they look at me like that, Mama?"

"Because you're special," I said. "Now, pray that there's a sale on in the fruit aisle and I'll buy some extra bananas."

· · ·

When Mary's cast came off, the children celebrated. My daughter, Sharon, made her a flower tiara from daisies and ivy, and they sang a song thanking God. It was a sign to me that I needed to have an open heart, like them, and I committed to myself and the Lord that I would forgive Ruth-Anne for striking my child and treat her with the same generosity of spirit that Clara showed me. Unfortunately, God had other plans.

The sun was sinking, and the hills that surrounded our compound turned a delicious, gold-tinged pink. Even the graveyard looked romantic, its simple tombstones brushed with marmalade hues. I was feeling more positive than I had in ages, and after helping Clara prepare the evening meal, I skipped outside to tidy up the toys the children had left in the garden. Ruth-Anne was supposed to be bathing them, but I saw her in the yard with Malachi and Becky, Clara's four-year-old twins. The three of them were crouching over, studying something. I guessed it was some plant or animal, and I let them be. I tidied the sandpit and pulled over the tarpaulin to protect it from the elements (and Smarticus) and wheeled a couple of bikes to the bike rack.

"Mom!" said Malachi, Clara's son. I had a soft spot for him, and I liked it when he called me *Mom*. Not all the kids did, even though Angus insisted.

"Mom!" he said again. "Come look here!"

Ruth-Anne looked up at me and smiled. It was almost dark, but the moon was bright. The valley we lived in always felt closer to the stars than anywhere else in the world. I took a moment to breathe in the beauty and to enjoy the peace in my heart, then walked over to them with a wide smile. I approached with caution, hoping it wasn't a snake or a spider.

Malachi pointed a gun at me. I recognised it immediately as Angus's revolver, which was kept in the family safe and only to be taken out in true emergencies. I wanted to think it was a toy, but we didn't allow play weapons. Malachi aimed it at me and pulled the trigger.

"Bang! Bang!" he said. I flinched, and he laughed. "Got you, Mom. I shot you dead."

I wrenched the gun away from him with shaking hands.

"What is WRONG with you?" I demanded, first of Malachi, and then Ruth-Anne.

Malachi looked hurt.

"We were just playing with it," said Becky.

Adrenaline was flooding my body. My shaking worsened, the gun bouncing in my hands.

"What is wrong with you?" I asked Ruth-Anne. "Are you INSANE?"

Ruth-Anne laughed in that way that irritated me so much. Brashly, loudly, as if hurling an insult through the air. "Relax," she said. "It's not loaded."

I clicked open the barrel and checked. There were no bullets.

"Get inside," I told the twins. When they tried to argue with me, I cut them down with a searing stare. I left Ruth-Anne standing there in the dark and marched straight to Angus.

"I want her out of this house," I seethed. All the kindness and compassion I had been cultivating flew straight out of the window. "Either she goes, or I do."

"This is extremely upsetting," said Angus, checking the gun and putting it back into the safe. I saw him change the password. "This is just a terrible thing."

"I'm sincere, Angus," I said. "If you choose her, I'm leaving. And I'm taking my children with me."

"Please," said Angus. "I can see you're upset. I am, too."

"Malachi could have shot Becky," I said. "He could have shot me."

"God has spared your lives."

"God wouldn't have had to spare our lives if Ruth-Anne hadn't put us in danger!" I was shouting, and I didn't care.

"This is something we can work through as a family," said Angus. "It's a teachable moment for Ruth-Anne."

"Angus," I said, and my body shook all over like I had never experienced before. "I'll be packing my bags tonight."

"Please," said Angus. "Don't do this."

I stabbed my chest with my finger. "*I* am not doing this. *I* am not doing any of this. Ruth-Anne is doing it. She's been a force for destruction since the moment we met her."

That is indeed how I saw her: a dark tornado that would soon raze our house and everyone in it. Angus could stand by and watch if he wanted to, but I was going to save my children.

Angus and Ruth-Anne had a noisy argument. Ruth-Anne had no qualms about shouting at Angus, which was the only thing I liked about her. We heard snippets of the fight through the walls, and some of the smaller children cried.

Clara watched me pack, begging me to reconsider.

"I'll think of something," she said. "I'll keep us safe."

"You can't!" I said, zipping a bag closed. It was difficult to pack when my vision was awash with tears, but I had made up my mind. I kept imagining what would have happened if there had been bullets in the gun.

"Hannah!" she shouted, and I snapped out of my emotional blaze and dropped the bag. I collapsed onto the floor and began to weep. Clara kneeled and embraced me.

"Don't leave me," she said. "I love you. I'll always love you."

We hugged harder than ever until the tension left my body, and I was exhausted. Then she put me to bed and tucked me in as if I were one of her children.

I didn't see Ruth-Anne the next day, or the next. When I asked the children, they said she was sleeping. Maybe she felt bad about what had happened, or perhaps she had some kind of psychotic break. I was glad not to see her. Clara dutifully took her meals three times a day on the dinner tray decorated with farmhouse animals. Most of the meals came back untouched, but Clara was not discouraged. On the third day, she made her famous chicken broth served with freshly baked bread, and the bowl came back empty. My bags were still packed. I hadn't yet decided if I was going to follow through with my plan to leave. We already did so much work for so little money. Perhaps a job in a nice town somewhere would be better? But then I'd gaze at Clara and our children, and I couldn't imagine a life without her.

In the middle of the night I stole into her bed and snuggled into her. "I love you," I said, and she kissed me.

Seeing as though the chicken broth was the only thing that Ruth-Anne would eat, we made a huge pot of it for the week and stored it in the cool room. The children were told not to touch it. With forgiveness and patience I admired, Clara warmed a portion of soup every mealtime for Ruth-Anne. She bathed her and dressed her in clean pyjamas, and spent hours reading scriptures to her. Despite the care being shown, Ruth-Anne's condition worsened. Soon she complained about loud noises when there were none, and said her body was afflicted with pins and needles. Her skin had an awful colour—cooked oats—and her hair began to fall out.

"She needs a doctor," Clara and I said to Angus.

"Leave it in the hands of God," he said.

"What if we had left Mary's broken arm in God's hands?" I asked. I had by then become more forceful in my dealings with my husband. I had stayed quiet for too long, not causing trouble, not making a fuss, not rocking the boat.

"Mary's arm was broken," said Angus. "Ruth-Anne just needs our prayers."

Clara and the children prayed by her side, asking God to heal her disquieted mind. Some days she would seem better, and I became suspicious that she was feigning her illness to avoid housework, but then a day or two later she'd be cold and sweating, or vomiting into the bucket beside her bed.

"She's getting worse," Clara peeled off the rubber gloves she had been wearing to scrub Ruth-Anne's bathroom. She smelled of bleach.

Clara called a family meeting. "She should be at the hospital. Her condition is deteriorating."

"Ruth-Anne will be well again in time," said Angus. "Perhaps this is the Almighty's way of allowing her time to consider her behaviour."

"You think God is punishing her?" I asked. The thought had occurred to me, too.

"I cannot say what our Lord's intentions are," said Angus. "I can only say that His will is my command."

We prayed together, then moved to our rooms. Clara helped me unpack my bags.

Ruth-Anne continued her downward spiral. We intensified our prayers and readings from the Scripture. The pastor came by to bless Ruth-Anne and give her the holy sacrament. Just like I had felt my happiness slipping away when Angus and Ruth-Anne became engaged, now I felt Ruth-Anne's life slipping away.

"Shall we just put her in the truck?" I whispered to Clara. "We can take her to the hospital before anyone knows what we've done."

"We'll be excommunicated," said Clara. "It is not our way. Angus has spoken, and it is in the hands of God. Besides, Ruth-Anne should be with her own people at a time like this. You know that the others are like. They don't understand us."

I still thought I should just take her, but then I remembered the judgmental looks we got while shopping, the questions, the interrogating stares. I couldn't imagine Ruth-Anne staying in a hospital with all those strange, suspicious people around her. There was more chance of her getting better in her own bed, surrounded by love.

Clara, exhausted by an all-night prayer vigil the night before, fell asleep before lunch-time, so I let her rest, fed the kids, and went to fetch some chicken broth to warm for Ruth-Anne. When I opened the door to the cool room, an empty porcelain bowl in my hands, I saw that our greedy tabby, Smarticus, was lying in the corner.

"Oh, you naughty cat," I said affectionately. "How did you get locked in here?"

Smarticus was an expert at stealing fresh cream from the pail. When he didn't move, I walked over to pet him. As soon as I touched his fur, I drew back with a gasp and dropped the bowl. It smashed on the cold concrete beneath me. I began blinking rapidly, perhaps from the shock, and was about to call for Clara when I remembered she was asleep. I touched Smarty again, and recoiled again. His body was already stiff.

I looked at the container of chicken broth and saw the tell-tale signs of feline tampering. The cat had managed to help himself to some of Clara's famous chicken broth.

My heart was hammering as I swept up the shards of porcelain and binned them. I fetched an old frayed towel and wrapped Smarticus up, carrying his small body like a baby. I took him outside where I buried him in our family graveyard, where we'd all end up one day. The people not of our faith didn't like it, but we didn't register births or deaths in our compound. Our leaders said it was no-one's business but our own.

I watched the sky as it turned from blue to pink to fiery orange, and I decided to leave the matter of Clara's chicken broth in the hands of God.

∿

DEAR READER

Thank you for staying with me on this journey!

I love hearing from readers, so please don't hesitate to get in touch. I'm only an email away!

I'd especially like to know which story was your favourite, and if there are any in particular you'd like to see turned into novels.

If you'd like to read more disturbing short stories, my next collection, Sticky Fingers 6, is available to order. You'll see that they're as unsettling as ever.

∽

"Lawrence makes every word count, telling each story with elegance and emotional punch." — Patsy Hennessey

"Each story is masterfully constructed ... Humorous, touching, creepy, but most of all entertaining, this collection is superb." — Tracy Michelle Anderson

Dear Reader

Thank you for supporting my work!

Janita

www.jt-lawrence.com

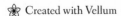

Made in the USA
Monee, IL
31 July 2021

74634271R00132